WHEN THE OX CARRIES THE ARK

Andrew Robert

Copyright © 2023 **Andrew Robert Publishing**

All rights reserved. No part of this publication may be reproduced, distributed, or transmitted in any form or by any means, including photocopying, recording, or other electronic or mechanical methods, without the prior written permission of the publisher, except in the case of brief quotations embodied in critical reviews and certain other noncommercial uses permitted by copyright law. For permission requests, write to the publisher, addressed "Attention: Book Rights and Permission," at the address below.

Published in the United States of America

ISBN 978-1-960159-98-4 (SC)

Andrew Robert Publishing
222 West 6th Street
Suite 400, San Pedro, CA, 90731
andrewrt120@hotmail.com

Order Information and Rights Permission:

Quantity sales. Special discounts might be available on quantity purchases by corporations, associations, and others. For details, contact the publisher at the address above.

For Book Rights Adaptation and other Rights Permission. Call us at toll-free 1-888-945-8513 or send us an email at admin@stellarliterary.com.

About the Book

When the ox carries the Ark is a Scriptural meeting point of world politics and leadership.

It unravels the Biblical parables, connects it to our today's politics and traits among leaders.

In this book, you will find Andrew Robert's personal message to President Joe Biden as divinely revealed to him as regard his emergence as the 46th American president.

When the ox carries the Ark is capable of causing a radical change that can positively transform any nation or institution.

Nations are not in lack of wealthy resources to elevate her citizens, but they're in lack of witty leaders. The prosperity of any nation equals the witty state of her leaders. When the ox carries the Ark, even your precious gold will be turned into worthless dust. One of the greatest disservice on earth is the attitude of maintaining a harmful Status quo. After reading this book, don't stand on the wrong side or play neutrality, rather act to make things better in the areas of your influence.

Table of Contents

About the book iii

Chapter One	And Five Were Wise, And Five Were Foolish	1
Chapter Two	When The Ox Carries The Ark	9
Chapter Three	Uzzah Is Dead	18
Chapter Four	Cows Of Bashan On The Hill	20
Chapter Five	Imbalanced Scale	31
Chapter Six	Aged With Savant & Sage	35
Chapter Seven	Repairing The Broken Bridge	42
Chapter Eight	The Power Of Unity	46
Chapter Nine	Bridge The Gap By Innovation	52
Chapter Ten	History And Lesson To Learn	59
Chapter Eleven	How Jesus Dealt With Corruption	64
Chapter Twelve	The Fig Tree	71
Chapter Thirteen	Dealing With The Figs!	76
Chapter Fourteen	Nathaniel, Innocent Victim!	79

Message To President Joe Biden 83

Chapter Fifteen	Cure For The Plague	89

About the Author 96

WELCOME TO
WHEN THE OX CARRIES THE ARK II

Every human activity in all spheres of life, whether they are spiritual or physical exists to authenticate the truth of God's spoken Word. This book identifies politics as a human system within the ambits of God's word. The Word of God is all encompassing, firm, settled and ideologies. These ideologies therefore have to align with the core message and values of the living God- 'a message of God's outmost desire for total inclusiveness.' God is for all human race and God is not religious. The Bible is not just a Christian book as some might want to believe, but God's instruction manual for human guidance.

I want to use this medium to appreciate every leader who has shown class and character in their various capacities around the world. May posterity remember your good work and sacrifice!

How do we explain this? Two countries: one filled with human and natural resources and the other, not so endowed yet the not-so-endowed country overtakes the other country with unimaginable strides in every imaginable positive sphere? The answer is simple, one is being led by visionaries and another is being led by corrupt and visionless leaders. This is probably the best way to describe Nigeria and many African countries in comparison to the likes of Singapore, Malaysia, Thailand, Vietnam, Indonesia, India and several other Asian countries including Taiwan and mainland China.

"Do not be deceived, God is not mocked; for whatever a man sows, that he will also reap" Galatians 6:7 (NKJV)

The earth is called mother earth because just like a mother's womb, the earth reproduces whatever seed you sow into it and gives it back to you in a bigger measure. So, in terms of gender case, nations are referred to in feminine terms. Correspondingly therefore, if a leader sows prosperity, the nation will reap prosperity in return. And, if a leader sows corruption, the land will also see a multiplied measure of corruption. The aforementioned nations and other prospering nations had in times past sown seeds of prosperity, and over time are reaping what their founding leaders sowed.

Chapter One
AND FIVE WERE WISE, AND FIVE WERE FOOLISH

Then shall the Kingdom of heaven be likened unto ten virgins, which took their lamps, and went forth to meet the bridegroom. And five were wise, and five were foolish (Matthew 25:1-2)

The word fool is used for "someone with poor judgment, understanding or little intelligence."

Abraham Lincoln said, "It's better to remain silent and be thought a fool than to speak and remove all doubt."

In Proverbs 17: 28 the Bible says, "Even a fool, when he holds his peace is considered wise."

Holding their peace connotes staying out of public space in sensible matters and decisions.

Anytime we watch the Olympic opening ceremonies, and see representatives of the participating countries each with their touch, I am always reminded that, the essence of the touch is the desire to shine during the Olympic Games as representatives of their respective nations. So, countries do ensure they are represented by their best.

Likewise, every family, organization, and institution have their touch or lamp bearers. In the event of an Olympic, it will be a monumental stigma for a country's touch bearer to get exhausted or stop half way into the rally without getting to the finish line. The country's would feel grieved, and regret their choice of representative at such an event. I'm sure that any nation with honor would be careful to trust any man who has badly represented them at a previous similar event, because doing so would be liken to one trusting his life savings or family assets to an institution that is bound to crash or go bankrupt.

Many people are victims of this, when they entrust our life to people based on empty promises or how they appear. These are people who come with lamps in their hand without fuel to light it up. We have over the years embraced people who come with lamps in their hands but end up plunging nations, organizations, institutions, even families and individuals into darkness. God Himself feels displeased with such persons who fail in their promises because He desires us to stay true to our words or promises.

In the Bible says, "Let your yes be yes or let your no be no' anything beyond this is from the evil one." (Matthew 5:37) In essence, He wants us to faithfully commit to what we say or the promises we make especially when those we promised faithfully do their bid. Promises that gets people to yield and place their hope on what we say is like a vow, breaking the promises is offensive before God (Ecclesiastes 5:4, Romans 1:31).

The word of God in the above referenced Scripture, 'Ecclesiastes 5:4' says "When you vow, pay what you vow for God has no pleasure in a fool." You make a fool of yourself when you fail in your promises. We have seen politicians deny the promises they made during campaigns after they entered into office. This fact characterizes Muhammadu Buhari's regime, because his administration appears to be bereft of ideas and the will needed to bring about the fulfillment of their promises.

Lamps without Light

When Jesus spoke about the five foolish and five wise virgins in Matthew 25:2, He used oil and lamp as an illustration in His message. What does this connote? When we talk about Lamp, it simply speaks of **a device that gives or produces light.** It means anything that can be harnessed to remedy or deliver men from darkness, ensuring their wellbeing and brightness of life such as, "education and skill acquisition." Natural resources are lamps that are meant to harness and light up. In Ecclesiastes 5:9, the Bible calls it the profit of the earth. You don't make profit from a fallow earth; you bring profit out of what your do with the earth. So much is deposited beneath the earth that needs light to be revealed and delivered to humanity. The purpose of it all is to elevate and deliver men from wallowing in darkness or hopelessness. Light reveals things that are hidden from men.

The light of the gospel of Christ

Above the aforementioned examples, the gospel of Christ is the greatest lamp that brings brightness to one's total being if worked on. "Thy Word is a lamp unto my feet, and a light unto my path" Psalms 119:105.

In 2 Corinthians 4:3 the Bible says, "But if our gospel is hidden, it is hidden to them that are lost."

If this great treasure the "gospel" of Jesus Christ that is eternal, and far richer than silver, gold, or any earthly treasure you can imagine is hidden from you, it is because your spirit man has not aligned with God's Spirit. In 2 Corinthians 4 verse 4, the Bible says, "The god of this age has blinded the minds of such individuals, so that they would not see the light of the gospel that displays the glory of Christ, who is the image of God. In verse 6 it says, "For God, who said, "Let light shine out of darkness," made his light shine in our hearts to give us the light of the knowledge of God's glory displayed in the face of Christ".

Christ is the content of the gospel. And we can clearly see that within or in the gospel of Christ, is the light to liberate men from any form of darkness. The gospel is given to serve as light to humanity. In the gospel of Christ Jesus, the light of God is revealed to liberate those who receive it in truth.

Light is referred to as "illumination, information, knowledge, discovery, solution or a positive answer to a need. For clarity purpose, I want us to breakdown the first two words (illumination and information).

Illumination: the advanced oxford dictionary defines **illumination** as, "decoration of lights, usually colored lights." When you have light, you are decorated with **colors**, plural. This speaks of diversities of ideas, information and possibilities at the beck and call of such a one with light.

Information: to be informed is "to have data, obtain facts or communicable knowledge." This explains why dictators or an authoritarian leader operates in total contrast to the definitions of light or exposure to information. They take away access to information from their subjects/ citizens by fighting the press and every media that does not support their agenda. Every avenue through which citizens of such countries can access information is usually blocked because in learning is light or information that can bring about revolution into freedom.

In the same vein, as Christ is the content of the gospel, so is the oil to the lamp. No matter how fancy or attractive a lamp may appear, it is useless without the oil to light it up.

In our key Scripture Matthew 25 Verse 2, "Five were wise and five were foolish." What made the five foolish was not because they refused to be amongst the other wise virgins, not because they were not involved in the activities with other wise virgins, and it wasn't because they were not tutored or obedient to the conventional rules, neither were they foolish because they had no lamps, "**But they were foolish because they lacked oil or fuel in their lamps.**"

An engine requires oil to run. Oil is the first thing to check before an engine is started to embark on a journey. In addition to this, an engine without oil is bound to crack. How does this apply to us? Just like lamps and engines need oil to run, we very much need oil if our light must not go off. Oil or fuel in this context is a metaphoric word used by Jesus to drive home His point. He was not in any way particular about literal oil or fuel. Fuel here speaks of energy, power, capacity or a driving force. Like engines and lamps that need fuel to run, everyone has their driving force. Having the lamps is having the physical qualification, but your physical qualification cannot take you to the point of your destination, your character will. Your oil or fuel is your inner quality, that's your character or attitude. King Saul had the feature of a lamp in his physical attribute because he was the most favored in appearance but he lacked oil inside. On the other hand, king David had oil but lacked in the beautiful appearance of Saul.

There are many nations of the world and Africa in particular which are far behind in development because rulers having lamp without oil, are leading the affairs of these nations. This is so because anyone having the lamp has the responsibility to lighten the path for those they lead to walk in brightness. These five virgins could not turn on their lamps when duty called, and consequently were shutout.

Virgin, as used in that scripture, is a metaphorical term for undefiled or uncorrupted persons. It is a great thing to be identified as a virgin, that is, to be seen as undefiled or uncorrupted. This is certainly a good (lamp image) that is often projected by politicians to lure the masses into believing their political sermon. But so often, many of these men don't have the oil required to light up people's lives. Remember, oil is your energy, light, ideas, information, and all the characteristics that befit a leader.

When one has the lamp, it is normal for people to look up to him with expectations. But when at night hours (challenges), the lamp carrier fails to turn it on, people's hope and expectations are bruised. There's a great danger when one who is expected to lead lacks ideas or vision. There's a great distress when people's expectations are cut short because those they trusted to lead cannot light up the lamp. In the absence of vision, destruction is eminent Proverbs 29:18.

To better understand the context of this Scripture Matthew Chapter 25 and its core message of "Five wise and five foolish virgins," we must look back at the preceding message in chapter 24.

In Chapter 24 of Matthew, Jesus was teaching about the signs of the end time. I want us to take a critical look at the statement of Jesus in this chapter. In every sphere of life, when the end is coming there are always indicating signs. For example, before a nation is plunged into economic recession or into chaos, there're signs, before any disaster happens, there're signs and before any relationship, business or organization disintegrates there will be signs too.

When you read Matthew Chapter 24, you will observe that Jesus went from highlighting on the events of the end time to talking about "faithful wise servants and evil servants". Why the placements of servants in this scenario? It is simple; Jesus doesn't want people to loom in darkness or uncertainty in the face of unprecedented events. He wants people to be guided and enlightened in the truth that should make them free from doom. And to be delivered from such, there must be a watchman or a lamp bearer otherwise referred to as servants in the context of Matthew 24. These servants or stewards must have good understanding of the essence of their position which is to nourish their subjects and guide them in light so they can be delivered from destruction.

Matthew 24:45-47 "Who then is a faithful and wise servant, whom his master made ruler over his household, to give them food in due season? Blessed is that servant whom his master, when he comes, will find so doing. Assuredly, I say to you that he will make him ruler over all his goods" (NKJV).

The first thing we should take from this scripture is that **leaders are stewards or servants**. This is not man's idea but God's.

Leadership responsibility is well defined in this scripture. The leaders are to feed their subjects with knowledge, upgrade them with information, guide them on moral issues and empower them for prosperity.

Matthew 24:48-51 "But if that evil servant says in his heart, 'My master is delaying his coming, and begins to beat his fellow servants, and to eat and drink with the drunkards, the master of that servant will come on a day when he is not looking for him and at an hour that he is not aware of, and will cut him in two and appoint him his portion with the hypocrites. There shall be weeping and gnashing of teeth" (NKJV).

The evil servant says in his heart, my master is delaying, and he began to beat his fellow servants, and began to eat and drink. The master in the context of this Scripture is God who is the creator of all things. And the servant or stewards of the house are leaders in their various capacities, while fellow servants are their subjects.

Nothing takes God unaware, God sees through the heart. So, there's no question as to whether He knew the steward would fail his fellow servants or not, God knew.

But we don't usually have the full knowledge of the inner components of most people we elect as public servants because, until they become it, they appear as lambs.

Evil servants as the Bible calls them know how to disguise. They are perfect in playing the game of saints that they are not. They present beautiful lamps without oil just to gain their ways up, but once they're in, they'll begin to beat those they ought to have fed and they'll begin to eat and drink.

They were supposed to be servants but once in power, they become power drunk and abusive. This is the torture many around the world are subjected to particularly in Africa; people have been beaten down by those entrusted to feed them. Africans are beaten into poverty and hardship, beaten to obscurity and into losing their self-worth, beaten down with depravity. The master has given us all things for the good of all, but the evil steward has taken it all to himself.

But I pray for divine intervention, that the light in your family, nation and organization will not go off before God raises your Samuel to rescue and lighten up what's dying (I Samuel 3:3&4).

Chapter Two
WHEN THE OX CARRIES THE ARK

Like other animals, there are many ox species. They come with deferent names like "cattle, bull, cow", etc. An ox is a multipurpose animal that is used for ploughing, goods conveyance and transportation. Because of its tamable nature and great energy, the ox has been used for centuries in many parts of Asia, Africa and around the world for day to day activities.

Just as chickens cannot fly as high as the eagle, it is also very important to understand that an ox has its limits. Due to its strength and multipurpose value, some have assigned the ox duties outside its jurisdiction thereby ending up in great jeopardy.

Despite the ox's strength and men's ability to tame it, it has extreme poor memory, a very poor vision, little or no intelligence or sense of sound judgment. The severity of its poor sight and sense of judgment is so bad that an ox would rather attack a moving and harmless object in closer proximity than a lion. Take an ox a million times on a route, it will not be able to navigate the same route on its own. It is in its nature to stray from good paths. An ox can lay on the highway where heavy-duty vehicles ply defying all sense of safety.

In the context of this title, "When the Ox carries the Ark," it is important to have a paradigm understanding of an ark, or better known as (The Ark of the Covenant) as recorded in the scriptures.

Ark

An ark is a box built for the purpose of preserving something of great value. The first mention of an ark in the Bible was in Genesis 6:14 and it was for the preservation of lives. God had instructed Noah to build the Ark of safety against an impending flood that eventually destroyed that generation.

And the second time God instructed an ark to be built, it was also for the preservation of the nation of Israel. Spare me for the long narration on how Jacob and his children went to Egypt, in fulfillment of God's word to Abraham their father in Genesis 15:13. God had revealed that his children would be strangers in another land for 400 years. While in Egypt, it took them an extra 30 years to align with God's time frame of 400 years, so they ended staying in Egypt for 430 years. After 430 years in Egypt, God miraculously brought Israel out of Egypt by the hand of Moses. After their deliverance, God instructed Moses to build the Ark of the Covenant.

In the Book of II Samuel 6 Verse 2, the Ark is called by the name, "The Lord of Host." To be a host is to accommodate a person or group of persons. The guest's total wellbeing is the responsibility of his or her host. The Ark of the Covenant was the presence of God amongst the Israelites as 'The Host' watching over them. It was their strength, stronger than any power. And it was their wealth, richer than oil and gas or any gold and diamond field, it was their needed surplus and help for every need, and it was their light in dark moments.

In Deuteronomy 10:8, God instructed that the ark should be carried by the priests. As long as Israel's camp kept good judgments doing what was right, God was to defend them and the ark (which was the presence of God) was the means for their victory. Remember, all the great benefits of the ark were only guaranteed as long as Israel kept the divine ordinance. The same is true with humans and any nation! There is no one on earth created empty and no nation on earth without a natural deposit within its shore. Any resource that God deposits in any one or any nation's shore that is not rightly managed becomes a snare. The wrong use of Balaam's prophetic gift and the wrong use of Ahithophel's gift became their snare. It is recorded in the Bible that during the days of Eli, the leaders of the nation of Israel declined into moral decay, and their acts became abhorrent to The Lord of Host. Consequently, the land became polluted for The Holy Lord of Host, and His covering presence and power was made of no effect because of their evil. Therefore, and sadly too, the Ark could not save them when they came under attack by the Philistines.

Again, the same is true when there is leadership failure, the effect of the nation's wealth and rich resources will not reflect in the lives of the citizens. The Bible says in first Samuel two verse twelve that "the sons of Eli were corrupt, and did not know God." These sons of Eli were the priests, and leaders of the nation of Israel. The position of the sons of Eli was clear, to teach the nation the precepts and ordinances of God. They carried the Ark of God, yet they didn't know God. What a dilemma! Leaders of a nation ruled by God's principles didn't know God. In many of their corrupt acts, they took their choice portions of the daily sacrifices rather than the prescribed portion commanded by

God for the priests. The same is true with our leaders today, lacking all sense of leadership quality like the sons of Eli. Corrupt with impunity, and extreme ignorance of the law and constitution. They go beyond their allowances and salaries to plunder public treasuries without mercy.

The nation of Israel was in battle with their Philistine neighbor, Israel went to battle without the Ark and the hands of the Philistines prevailed over them. Israel immediately turned to their great strength, the Ark to tackle their enemy. The Ark of God was brought into the frontline by the priests who do not know God nor understand the order of the Ark. When the Ark was brought, there was a thunderous noise of jubilation in the camp of Israel, "Yes, the Mighty God has arrived to aid us into victory." The jubilations we had seen among Africans and 3rd world leaders when they discover lucrative solid minerals like oil and gas, gold or diamond field. Not knowing that it is worse to have a mismanaged resource than not having at all.

Proverbs 29: 2 says, "When the righteous (the right people) are in authority, the people rejoice, but when the wicked rules, the people grieve."

When the Philistines understood that Israel's shouting was in celebration of the ark, they were frightened and in disarray as they cried, "Woe to us! Who will deliver us from the hand of these mighty Gods? These are the Gods who struck the Egyptians with all the plagues in the wilderness" (I Samuel 4:7-8).

This is very common among visionless leaders, their minds are so much programmed on oil, gold or diamond sales to run their economy, whenever their neighboring country discovers any profitable resources, they feel bad wishing the resource was theirs. But often, those countries with prospective edge fail. They fail because it is not about what you have, but about who manages what you have as was the case of Israel under Eli and his son's leadership. Under their leadership, Israel ended in defeat to their seemingly weak Philistine neighbor.

The leaders of Israel had failed in their responsibility to God's displeasure and so, the Ark of the Covenant could not deliver them.

The Philistines prevailed over Israel and at this time, Israel's power base "the Ark" was captured. The Philistines approach was similar to any super power's approach in capturing nations during invasion. Whenever a super power nation subdues another nation, they take over their power base and capture their treasury.

The Philistines captured the ark, the glory departed and the nation of Israel was plunged into what would be a tough period of their history since leaving Egypt. Any great nation's glory can be stripped if run by visionless leaders like Eli and his sons (cabinets).

The ark was taken to the land of Philistine with great celebration! But what the Philistines did not know was that the Ark of the Covenant is not like Dagon, 'the Philistines demonic idol.' The ark was taken to the house of Dagon, and it didn't take long before the ark began to plague the whole land of the Philistine. This also proves that the glory of the Ark in itself never diminishes, but rather needs the right minds to manage it.

The lords of the Philistines summoned their idol priests and diviners to enquire the cause of their plague. And they were told that the Ark of God in their land was the cause. And that the land can only be freed if the ark is returned to Israel. The lords of the Philistine were instructed that to return the ark, they should get two cows (oxen), make a cart and let the oxen carry the ark back to Israel.

Following the instructions of their demonic idol priest, the ark was put on oxen and it was returned to Israel. The ark is back in Israel, the Philistines can now breathe with a sigh of relief that the cause of their plague was gone. On the other hand, the Israelites who were once bowed in shame because of the departed glory (the Ark), were in celebration because their strength was back.

When the ox carries the ark

There's a saying that goes thus, "Let the cap be on the head it fits the most." In truth, the cap of leadership is not fitting on the ox. The consequence of projecting an ox as a human deliverer has been catastrophic. In the Book of Exodus Chapter 32, after the children of Israel left Egypt and crossed the red sea, God instructed Moses to come up the mountain to receive the law. While he was on the mountain, the children of Israel cried to Aaron to give them a leader hence Moses was nowhere within their sight. In other to impress the people, Aaron thought of nothing else to present to them rather than an ox as their god. Remember God is against the worship of any image including angelic images. But pause for a while and think, of all creatures and animals such as lions, eagles, elephants, tigers or even the apes, none of these smart animals occurred to Aaron to present to Israel except for an ox!

Projecting an ox as leaders is not the desire of God for any nation, because it comes with negative and severe consequences as was the case with Israel.

[1] It comes with economic wreck!

Before they left Egypt, God gave Israel favor in the sight of the Egyptians. They came out with wealth in abundant of gold. Sadly, they lost most of that wealth as Moses grinded and dumped their gold in a deep river beyond their reach when the golden ox idol was projected as their deliverer. When an ox is projected to take over leadership, the nation's wealth comes under the risk of ruin.

[2] People are disunited!

Exodus 32:26 "Then Moses stood in the entrance of the camp, and said, 'Whoever is on the Lord's side Let him come unto me!" And all the sons of Levi gathered themselves unto him. Then the camp was divided.

[3] The good in the land will not circulate to everyone.

In II Samuel 6: 10 & 11, due to Israels leadership error and fear, the ark was domiciled in the house of Obededom. The Bible records that because of its presence there, the house of Obededom was greatly blessed in all ramification. Obededom's house became the sole beneficiary of the divine provisions that ordinarily would have been the lot of the whole nation of Israel if the ark was carried by the priests and kept in its prescribed order.

This situation can be likened to the experiences of some African nations where the nation's wealth is accessed only by a few individuals- the ruling class. I pray that as the leaders of Israel retraced their steps and the ark was taken from the house of Obededom so that the entire nation would be blessed, our leaders would ensure by polices and goodwill, wealth dissemination in Nigeria and Africa.

[4] The land is polluted with blood!

Exodus 32:27 "..put every man his sword by his side, and go in and out from gate to gate throughout the camp and slay every man his brother, and every man his companion, and every man his neighbor.

[5] The nation is stagnated

If you study your Bible carefully, you would understand that the act of projecting an ox resulted in Israel's delay in entering the promised land. Moses returned to the mountain a second time for another 40 days. On his return, he implemented every instruction given to him by God in order to guide the nation against making the same mistake of projecting an ox.

As soft as this might sound, the weight and the negative effect of their error was monumental. Long after the people repented of their act of choosing an ox, they spent years on that spot of Sinai. This implies that after the ox era, navigating out of ox leadership damages would not come cheaply. With good leaders and leadership, after the nation is channeled on the right direction, it could take some years for them to cross their Sinai {challenges} before entering and enjoying their promised land.

[6] The people are naked [Exodus 32:25].

To be naked is to be stripped, unprotected, helpless, or vulnerable. Nigerian citizens are so vulnerable, unprotected and helpless like never before under Buhari's administration. The question people ask on a daily bases is not if there was an attack, but how many attacks, not if any was killed but how many were killed.

[7] The laws of the land are broken without consequence [Exodus 32:19].

When the ox leads, leaders and their subjects break the law without consequence. Under Buhari's regime, terrorist and bandits are being rewarded. Government negotiates jumbo settlements with criminals while law abiding citizens languish. Note that God did not query Moses for breaking the written law because the instant the nation of Israel accepted the ox leadership, the law became of no effect. Africa and third world political vile practices has nullified their moral constitution, they break the law and also reward their likeminded criminals.

In 1 Samuel Chapter 3 we saw how Eli and his sons lose the sense of leadership before the ark of God was captured by the Philistines. The same is true with many African countries today. For their vile attitude, many African countries have mortgaged their glory (ark), to a foreign country like China.

Tragically, under Buhari's led APC, these are woes that have befallen Nigeria. Bad enough that a minister under Buhari told Nigerians on tv that there's nothing wrong in Nigeria ceding her sovereignty to China. This was because Buhari's government sold Nigeria to China by taking unredeemable loans with a clause that will give China the Nations sovereignty if the terms are not kept. No one with human sense of reasoning would do such damage to his nation.

And to this end, I pray that every Ox like in our leadership space be rooted out.

Chapter Three
UZZAH IS DEAD

"When they came to the threshing floor of Nachon, Uzzah put out his hand to the Ark of God and took hold of it for the oxen stumbled. And the anger of the Lord burned against Uzzah and He struck him" (2 Samuel 6:6-7).

The ark that was supposed to save had become deadly. I have heard several sermons on the topic of Uzzah's death, describing him as one who tried to help God and got killed. That is not totally true because God doesn't operate on earth without a human vessel. Uzzah was a victim of leadership flaws. The ox has no business carrying the Ark, and the leaders of Israel ought to have known this. Long after the return of the ark from the land of Philistine in the days of Samuel, up until the days of Saul and David, the priests neglected their duty to carry the ark on their shoulders as commanded by God. Rather, they allowed the ark of God to be carried by an animal in a manner that was initiated by the demonic idol priests and diviners of the Philistine (oxen). And as the ark was being carried by the oxen, the oxen **stumbled** and Uzzah extended his hands to hold the falling ark, but sadly, he paid the ultimate price.

In Deuteronomy 11:26-28, God sternly warned that failure to adhere to divine order would turn blessings into curses. The problem was not the holding of the ark by Uzzah, but it was about the stumbling of the oxen.

From Uzzah's tragedy, we can clearly understand that whenever there's a leadership flaw, those that suffer the brunt are their subjects.

Today, many nations are stumbling because oxen or those lacking in sound judgment and vision are driving the ark of nations.

We are losing our Uzzahs, our frontline soldiers who are stretching their hands to protect our shores are dying. African leaders and their political appointees managing the affairs of our nations are stumbling, and those lending their hands to keep the nations from falling are the casualties we mourn daily.

Our wealth is being used by evil stewards to satisfy their evil greed. And the result of their cruelty in the land is pain, poverty and death from what should have been a blessing.

Psalm 106:20 says, "Thus they changed their glory into the similitude of an ox that eats grass."

The Scripture says they changed their glory to the likeness of an ox. They didn't change the glory of God, but their own glory.

One of the dictionary definitions of glory is '**optical,**' and one of the definitions of optical is 'sight or vision'.

No matter the height of a nation or how great an institution might be, when a leader with a poor vision like the ox leads, stumbling and catastrophe is inevitable. This can best explain why 3rd world and African countries, Nigeria in particular, is where she is today in spite of her rich minerals and great talents home and abroad.

Chapter Four
COWS OF BASHAN ON THE HILL

"For the creation waits in eager expectation for the children of God to be revealed" (Romans 8:19)

The above Scriptural Chapter and verse is my view on Africa as a continent. Until Africans get it right, the world will not be tranquil. There's a place in the heart and plan of God for Africa as prophesied by Isaiah in Chapter Nineteen of his book. The current state of Africa is far from its original destiny according to the plan of God. A continent blessed with so much, but in spite of her rich resources, the rest of the world sees Africa as a continent without content. This isn't the fact about Africa. Africa has suffered the effect of bad leadership. The continent's political structure has not allowed the best brains to function. It's been a politics of cash and carry, absolute power or bullying, subdue your opponents and win the elections regardless of the source of your wealth. The same thing Trump almost introduced into American politics.

Africans have the best brains academically. They are topnotch professionals in America, UK and other parts of the world where academic excellence is honored. But for safety and backlash, these smart men and women would rather pursue their careers quietly, yet with groanings and pains in their spirit as they watch their nation's affairs being piloted by oxen-like entities.

The rest of the world doesn't see or judge Africans by their individual achievements; they see and judge us by what they know about the continent.

There's a saying that "when good people refuse to act, evil happens." So often, when I see the actions of those in authority, and how it has negatively affected their subjects, I am left to wonder how wisdom has perish among those in high places.

Wisdom is the number one requirement for leadership. When Solomon asked God for wisdom, God was very pleased because he asked the right thing. Solomon's reign was at the time when king's domination was based on how many nations the king conquered. But Solomon did not engage in any battle, yet, his dominion was greater than those before him. There's no passing through life without battle, but in king Solomon's case, every looming battle cry was handled with Solomon's God given wisdom.

God created an angel called Lucifer, who became devil. God could have used His power and might to depose the devil of what he took from Adam but chose not, rather He used wisdom. In Matthew 28:18, After Christ's resurrection, He declared that "All power in heaven and on earth has been given to Him." Now, that power to reign and exercise dominion is resident in those who have Christ in them.

Through wisdom, God created all things and He reigns through wisdom. God created man and gave him dominion over all the earth. However, man's dominion was to be exercised through wisdom, not muscle. This is why Solomon's prayer for wisdom pleased God.

The wisdom of God is expressed in Christ, which is why the Bible says in I Corinthians Chapter One that He, "Christ" is the wisdom of God. Through Christ God created everything on earth and gave man "Adam" the dominion to reign over all.

God gave Adam a divine instruction that should be obeyed because in obeying that divine order was the authority derived to maintain the dominion He has graciously given to him (Genesis 1:26, Genesis 2:15-17, Genesis 3:4-7).

The very moment Adam disobeyed God and obeyed the devil, he became a slave to the devil. And everything that was under Adams control and all that was to come from his loins became subject to the devil because by law, whatsoever a slave has belonged to his master.

In order to restore the dominion back to anyone who will be willing to receive it, Christ had to come. He came not by the sinful blood of Adam that's flowing through the veins of every man born on earth. Christ came by the conception of the Holy Spirit by a virgin, in fulfillment of Isaiah's prophecy in Isaiah 7:14 & Matthew 1:23. This method of conception exempts Jesus from inheriting the Adamic sin. Without controversy, this makes Christ the only qualified savior and redeemer approved by the Almighty God. Christ came from heaven, humbled Himself in human form, suffered humiliation, pain and was hanged on the cross. He shed His blood by the foreknowledge of God to depose the devil of his dominion over God's creature. The Bible says in Philippians 2:5 "Let this mind be in you, which was also in Christ Jesus." The mind of humility even though all power and authority belong to Him. In verse 7, the Bible says "He made Himself of no reputation." In the process of dethroning the devil's authority, He did not exert or exercise His authority over anyone. In verse 8 of the same

Philippians 2, it says, "Being found in the fashion of a man, He humbled Himself, and became obedient unto death on the cross." This wisdom to reign is what every leader must crave for. No wonder the Bible says in 2 Corinthians 2:7-8 that had he, (the devil) knew it, he wouldn't have crucified the King of Glory, "Christ."

Through wisdom, God restored in Christ all that the devil took, and it came by His humility, sacrifice, love and all that is embedded in Christ. Therefore, Christ' life, character, sacrifice and death on the cross was a display of God's wisdom. This is why Christ is the wisdom of God.

Consequently, the only dominion that God approves is the dominion that is exercised through wisdom. If dominion is exercised through the use of power or force, it is regarded as oppression.

It wasn't a display of wisdom when President Buhari destroyed the image of Nigeria in his several trips overseas. A country that has given him so much, and the citizens he was elected to protect. He told the world that Nigerian youths are lazy, a statement made out of his ignorance and a proof of how disconnected he is from Nigerian youths. Nigerian youths are the most daring, adventurous and hardworking on the continent. It wasn't a display of wisdom when Buhari criminalized Nigerians in his lopsided fight against corruption before the outside world, scaring investors out of Nigerian shores.

It wasn't a display of wisdom when President Muhammad Buhari on his first overseas trip after being elected, told the world that the Igbos should not expect much from his government because they did not support his presidential bid.

I respect the right of anyone or group with a genuine reason to make a peaceful protest especially if they feel ill-treated. I still believe in one Nigeria in hope, but sometimes I wonder if Nigeria is truly One?

Though the Biafran agitation may not be constitutionally right, but the fight is morally right. Yes, morally right because of the unfair treatment they have been subjected to under Muhammadu Buhari's leadership. When the constitution fails to do justice, moral judgment takes its free course. There was no agitation until they were told by the president to the hearing of the whole world that they should not expect to benefit much from his government because they did not vote for him. A statement that can be interpreted as, 'the Igbos are not part of Nigeria,' the very height of segregation by supposedly the first citizen.

When the same people that were segregated against demanded for a referendum, armored tanks were rolled against them though they were armless civilians. They were oppressed, shot and left to swim in the pool of their blood.

Now these are the questions I can't find answers to: (1) Wasn't Buhari aware that Nigeria does not operate a one party system, and therefore there will be divergent votes? (2) As a leader isn't he supposed to build a bridge to prove oppositions and critics wrong and consequently win them over?

(3) Does he or anyone in his party have a private farm where the resources that run the country is cultivated? If the answer is no, how then can we be silent over such a conspiracy against a particular geographical region?

(4) I have not heard of any political leader or party in the past that gets support from all groups in the country. But after election and the tribunals that come with it, good leaders reach out to opposition groups because good leaders don't build walls, they build bridges.

In my curiosity to know why a president should make such a divisive statement, I went into President Buhari's archive, and what I discovered brought me to the conclusion that Buhari is nothing short of the ox as indicated in the title of this book, and a typical definition of this chapter, "Cow of Bashan on the Hill".

The mutual distrust and animosity between peoples of the Northern extraction and the Easterners led to the Nigerian civil war in 1967. The Igbos who are from the Eastern extraction felt aggrieved, and rightly so because they were the biggest losers of the war even though they had their share of blame in the events that led to the war. After the war, the leaders were able to get all the regions together and forge on as a nation. Thanks to the military head of state at the time, General Olusegun Obasanjo and those around him that brought the nation together in their wisdom. This unity led to Nigerian's first presidential election conducted by Olusegun Obasanjo in 1979 where Shehu Shagari from the North emerged as the winner with his Vice- Alex Ekwueme being from the East. This was the best thing that could happen in a country like Nigeria where trust was lost. A Northern President and his Eastern Vice President was the bridge and a sigh of relieve, mostly among the Eastern business-oriented nationals. The Igbos are known for their business adventures, and a united Nigeria was good for them to return to the North where they fled from during the war to restart their businesses. Sadly, the prospect of a more united Nigeria was put in jeopardy, when General Muhammadu Buhari unexpectedly overthrew Shagari and Alex Ekwueme's government in 1983 through a military coup.

The euphoric sense of one Nigeria was quickly put aside when Buhari arrested the ousted president Shehu Shagari and his Vice, Alex Ekwueme. Buhari sent the vice president from the eastern extraction to the most dreaded prison, and left Shehu Shagari, who incidentally is from the North in the comfort of his mansion and called it "a house arrest". This was perceived as a display of hate towards the Igbos, which consequently brought back their past grievance. It was no surprise therefore that those from the east had little or no regret when Buhari was eventually deposed by General Ibrahim Babangida on 27th August 1985.

In one of Ibrahim Babangida's interview, he was asked why he overthrew Muhammadu Buhari's government? In his response Babangida said "Buhari was too rigid in his attitude to issues." The word rigid is to be stiffed or lacking flexibility. That sounds so true because as they said, a leopard never changes its skin

Below is a report from "The New York Times" published in 1993 about Buhari.

"Moreover, there is a pervasive sense among Nigerian Christians that the military authorities favor the northern Islamic groups, who make up about half the country's 90 million people. Under Maj. Gen. Mohammed Buhari, General Babangida's predecessor, Christian schools were taken over by the state, and permits to build churches were held up while the construction of mosques increased." Link Source:

https://mobile.nytimes.com/1993/06/24/world/nigerian-military-rulers-annul-election.html

After nine years in power, Babangida conducted the infamous June 12th 1993 election. It was seen as the most successful and transparent election in Nigeria's history in which MKO Abiola emerged the winner of the presidential election. His victory was well received by most Nigerians and with high hopes, looking forward to having him in power to implement his promises. But to the bewilderment of everyone,

Babangida, on the 24th of June 1993, declared the election null and void. Home and abroad, Abiola was well loved and to a large extent, the election was transparent and peaceful. There was no explanation given on why the popular choice of a president by the people was jettisoned by Babangida. Babangida's regime was under tough criticism by the likes of Gani Fawehinmi of blessed memory, Professor Wole Soyinka and many others.

With international community's sanctions of all kinds placed on his government, General Babangida was pressured to announce he was stepping aside. Many were in doubt but this time, Babangida meant his word.

The best thing would have been to hand over to MKO Abiola, Babangida knew this, but a military general didn't want to be seen as a coward so he appointed a neutral face- Ernest Shonekan to man the affairs of the nation. Shonekan's time in office was short-lived because General Sani Abacha peacefully walked him out of office shortly after he was appointed interim President. That certainly didn't come as a big surprise to Nigerians, and of course Ernest Shonekan was not prepared for the office Babangida had ushered him into.

And once again, Nigerians were back to the military reign under a brutal and corrupt Abacha, who was ready to be a despotic ruler and even life-President. He used intimidation and arrest to silence those he considered threats including the former military head of state, Olusegun Obasanjo. Five years into his reign, Abacha died mysteriously while in office, paving the way for Abdulsalami Abubakar.

Giving the fact that Abdulsalami Abubakar was a serving military general of Northern extraction where people are said to be more power driven, and also taking into consideration the circumstances under which he came to power, a time when only military generals held sway in Nigeria, for him to have relinquished power is commendable.

After the 1993 MKO Abiola's election that was annulled by Ibrahim Babangida, most Nigerians were in doubt of democracy in the country. But that fear was laid to rest when Abdulsalami Abubakar faithfully kept to his promise, and conducted the elections that ushered Nigeria into the democracy the country is experiencing today.

He released all those who were incarcerated by Gen. Sani Abacha, notably 'Olusegun Obasanjo.' Olusegun Obasanjo who himself conducted the 1979 general election as a military head of state, won the presidential ticket to context under the umbrella of PDP (People Democratic Party). Olusegun Obasanjo was elected, and he justified his election to a good extent by carrying every section of the country along. This unity existed all through the 16 years of PDP's time in office until Buhari's government under the platform of APC (All Progressives Congress) began. And once again, in Buhari's characteristics of resentment and divisiveness, Nigerians are more divided than they have ever been in the history of the nation.

The essence of this long narrative and historical background is not to bring back the past, but to bring out the facts about those that have been carrying the ark of our nation and to let you judge their actions.

Your character and action define who you are. Criminals and terrorists have that name tagged on them because of their acts. When Nebuchadnezzar was behaving in an inhumane manner, he was made to live among beast, a fitting environment for his character.

Nebuchadnezzar at the time was oppressive towards the nations of the earth, taking kings and nations captive without restraint [Daniel 4:24-33]. When Herod was behaving wild, arresting and killing people, Jesus called him a fox. Foxes kill to survive and Herod was one who took pleasure in killing [Luke 13:32]. In Matthew 12:32, Jesus called the Scribes and Pharisees vipers because it was the definition of their deceptive and cunning character

In the book of Amos 4 verse 1, it says "**Hear this word, you cows of Bashan, who are on the mountain of Samaria, who oppress the poor, who crush the needy, who say to your husbands, "Bring wine, let us drink!"**"

[One], you cannot address a literal cow with such words as, "hear this word" as written in the verse above because literal cows do not understand human language.

[Two], literal cows do not live on the mountains.

[Three] literal cows do not oppress or crush people, neither do they consume wine. "**Cows of Bashan who are on the Mountain of Samaria**" speaks of those in high places of authority. Bashan was an ancient country that dealt shrewdly against Israel. Bashan's took over Samaria Israel's seat of power and treated the Israelites with cruelty.

There's a saying in Mexico that wings should not be given to scorpions to fly. Anyone who is power intoxicated, oppressive or acts senselessly is one Biblically regarded as a COW.

Having deprived the citizens socially, economically and politically, you still want to take their voices, a sign that the commander in chief and those around him are devoid of human senses.

The senseless killings and harassments of innocent citizens by a department in the Nigerian Police force called SARS was at its peak. Free and armless citizens came in mass to protest against the despicable acts of that department, but the government responded with rains of live bullets that left scores dead. Nigerians will never forget "The Lekki tollgate killing on October 20, 2020." The massacre of IPOB peaceful protesters, suppression of the press and intimidations of political opponents under Buhari's administration are perfect traits of Bashan cows on the hill.

As I conclude this chapter, may I tell you that most African leaders are oxen, because they are in the corridors of power using their privileged office for oppression…

Chapter Five
IMBALANCED SCALE

There was a debate over Buhari's attitude towards the Igbos. Some argued that his attitude towards them is a display of hate towards the Igbos. In his defense I remember his former running mate saying that Buhari's chef and driver are from the Eastern part, that Buhari doesn't hate them.

While I cannot dispute that, giving to the fact that I don't know Buhari's drivers or his cooks, but one known fact in Nigeria is, if you are a non-Yoruba, Hausa or Middle-belt residing in the West, or Northern parts, the Hausas and most Yorubas mistake you for Igbo. Some of them are ignorant of the fact that Nigeria does not only consist of Yoruba, Igbo and Hausa which are the three major ethnic groups. Nigeria has over 250 languages and those regarded as the minorities are the key components of the diversities Nigeria is known for. In view of this, it is possible that Tunde Bakare, the former running mate to President Buhari might have mistaken Buhari's chef for Igbo.

On the other hand, it is also possible to have someone from the East as Buhari's chef giving the fact that South East and her South-South neighbors have culinary skills and delicacies that are relatively well accepted nationwide. So, if a qualified chef from the East is employed to cook for Buhari, that cannot be considered a favor rather, it is a case of a man's gift making room for him.

Therefore, such an employment cannot be used as evidence to counteract his actions. One can draw conclusions from his actions.

In the Book of Proverbs 11:1 the Bible says, "A dishonest scale is abomination to the Lord, but a just weight is His delight."

A dishonest scale can be likened to creating an imbalance in a system. It is to place someone or group of persons in a position of disadvantage. Corruption is commonplace in our society because people no longer have balanced scales. A leader that understands the importance of comfort and that of his family, but denies those he is appointed to serve has lost their sense of balanced scales.

If God says an act is an abomination to Him, it will be evil to applaud or celebrate such acts from any leader. I am a Nigerian just like that Nigerian man, woman, boy or girl from Enugu, Osun, Sokoto, Benin, Ogoni land or anywhere else whether in the creeks or in the palace. I am a Nigerian. That is why I am crying out against this nepotism that has plagued the nation from inception. I am a Nigerian, I don't have to be from the East to cry out against the injustice melted on them by Buhari, I don't have to be a Tiv to cry out against the helplessness of the people of Benue and many others left at the hands of Fulani herdsmen and terrorists. I am a Nigerian and a world citizen. That is enough to cry out against the imbalanced scale used against certain groups who don't belong to the ruling party's wagon.

In the Nigerian Coat of Arms, it is written that the motto of Nigeria is "Unity and Faith, Peace and Progress".

After the 2015 presidential election that brought Buhari into office, on his first trip to Germany he told the world that the Igbos should not expect much from his government. That statement was a wanton display of imbalance and a threat to national unity.

When federalism fails, people lose faith and when people lose faith, they go in search of solace in their communities. This is the reason for agitations from different quarters under Buhari.

When in Buhari's ministerial appointments some sections were neglected to a large extent, that was imbalance.

When in the national budget under Buhari, some sections of the country receive less even though they are not the least in national wealth generation, that's imbalance.

When under Buhari, the North is favored more in recruitments in federal establishments, that's imbalance.

When in his early days of presidency, decisions were made in high places to place commodity importers which happened to be largely Igbos at a disadvantage, that was imbalance.

When IPOB (Indigenous People of Biafra's) nonviolent protest for what they perceived as oppression was met with security fire that left scores of people dead. Bear in mind that the aggression meted is far more than what the military has shown against the international terrorist groups in the North Eastern part of the country, that is imbalance.

When Buhari declared Biafran agitators a terrorist group, a group welding no arms, weapons or blood stain but refused to declare the obvious terrorist group (Fulani Herders) as terrorists, that was imbalance.

His stance therefore is that, IPOB is a visible terrorist group, whereas the heartless Fulani Herdsmen whose gory tales envelop the land are not terrorists even though their leaders are known. This only buttress the saying that "you give a dog a bad name so you can drown it".

If you can't see it you are not different from those who think killing others will make them stronger or stepping on others will make them rise higher.

If I have to worry or be cautious of my surroundings, it would be because of a friend who is dinning with my enemy.

The biggest obstacle to this battle against imbalance is not those from afar but from those within. the few who deny the reality of the pain inflicted upon the masses because of the slice of cake they enjoy from those oppressing their own people.

Chapter Six
AGED WITH SAVANT & SAGE

It is a fact that you cannot be yourself and at the same time be someone else, just as it impossible to be a youth and at the same time an elder. Equity demands that we treat others as we would love them treat us. No one would like to be told that he or she is unimportant. Prejudice or discrimination of any kind is a sin against humanity. Therefore, there should be space for everyone in the society the youth and the elderly. It is important we create balance and be rational in our judgment. A society that advocates the eradication of the elderly in their political and national affairs will have a king Rehoboam-like leadership experience.

When King Rehoboam, son of king Solomon took over from his father, he inherited his father's wise counselors but deliberately rejected their counsel and accepted the counsel of his friends and contemporaries who were youths. That action marked the beginning of the fall of his kingdom [1Kings 12:8].

Therefore, I don't believe that a nation's prosperity lies only with having youths at the helm of affairs. At the same time, there will be a disconnection between the youths that usually make up the larger percentage if the nation is completely governed by the elderly. If total leadership control is in the hands of the elderly who are not equipped with the data or relevant information for 21st century youths, it will be an open invitation for a revolution in any society.

In this computer age, a man who was vying for a political appointment was asked at the senate seating if he was IT friendly or computer literate. In his first response he asked, "What is IT?" He was then told that IT is an acronym for Information Technology. In his response, he said "gadgets are for young people like you" pointing to the senators. The question then is, why does someone who thinks he has outgrown IT and the use of modern innovative devices want to lead a generation that is IT compliant?

In the Book of Numbers Chapter 8 verse 25, the Old Testament priests with divine appointments were instructed to retire at fifty. Not because being over fifty makes one an antique, but it's because life is progressive and rigidity begins to set in once people exceed fifty. They become so traditional even to the detriment of progressive moves. It takes the grace of God and humility for those over fifty to learn or to be transformed to flow with new moves. In other to learn as an aged man, one must offload those outdated things in other to reload for the new move. This is the problem with most 3rd world politicians. They are too rigid in their opinions and quitting even in their failing state is never an option. They also see the privilege of leadership as a right or entitlement.

There're ordained leaders who are anointed with the leadership mantle even before they are born as is the case with Biblical Samson and Samuel. Despite the anointing on Samuel, Samuel still learned practical leadership under the tutorship of Eli. He witnessed how Eli's children were destroyed for their wrong acts and how their leadership failure plunged Israel as a nation into one of their darkest moments in history. He was able to filter the chaff from the wheat and this helped him to become one of the most successful leaders in Israel's history. On the other hand, Samson had no counselor or guidance to teach him wisdom and leadership virtues. And the Bible has the account of how he ended in an unpleasant manner despite the anointing on his life.

Savant and Sage! The word (savant) means "learning." That is "a person of learning, a teachable or versed person."

The word (sage) simply means "wisdom, or sound judgment." It will be unfair to insult or mock aged people because we all desire to enjoy the blessings of longevity. My point here is, since the world and life is progressive, anyone who desires to be relevant in leadership or in politics at old age must "age with savant and sage", "(ideas, information, wisdom and sense of sound judgment.)" This is the only way you can lead at old age. Not like the man who had a desire to lead yet blatantly told the Senate that he was above computer age.

The baton of good leadership and ethics should be something that our leaders ought to take delight in as they pass it on to the next generation. Unfortunately, not many African and 3rd world countries can boast of such good examples of leadership. This partly explains why there is a continuous circle of leadership flaws. The future of any country depends on the benevolent acts of our elder statesmen towards the younger leaders.

Eagle's example!

In Deuteronomy 32:11 the Bible says, "As the Eagle stirs up its nest, hovers over its young, spreading out its wings, taking them up, and carrying them on its wing."

There's a great virtue worth learning from eagles here.

When an eaglet is hatched, it remains in its nest until it is being stirred. What the eagle does is that, the eagle comes and stirs the nest, hovers over the eaglet, takes the eaglet up and spreads its wing to catch the eaglet. Though the eagle wants the eaglet to fly, she also understands the risk of inexperienced eaglets flying without the provision for safe landing. So, the eagle spreads her wings for the eaglet to fall on.

We have youths that should be given the needed help to fly, but there're all trapped in their nests with no one to stir them up. If by chance anyone is lifted, there's hardly any protective shield for our inexperienced youths to fall on in a case of policy- miscalculation. This has resulted in the falling and breaking of the few youths who have been opporture to work in top leadership positions.

Eagle's characteristics

Another quality the eagle has that sets it apart as the king of all birds is its vision.

The eagle's vision is so strong that it can pick something that is so microscopic. An eagle can see a fish beneath the water and grab it without missing it. Eagles can sight a little mouse miles away and have it clutched with its excellent maneuvering. Anyone who cannot see far has no business being in leadership.

Another strength that an eagle possesses is its wings. Eagles don't fly around, they mount high, using their vision in picking their prey and soar on the winds or current against what they have seen below and flap upward. Eagles flap less than other birds but fly higher than all. Eagles use the direction of the wind so it doesn't need to struggle to fly. The skill of the eagle is predicated on its understanding of the direction of the wind. I It is this hunting technics that makes the eagle one of the world deadliest predators.

What makes eagle such a formidable creature and a perfect example for us? Savant and sage!

In Isaiah 40:31 the Bible says, "They that wait on the Lord shall renew their strength, they shall mount up with wings as eagles, they shall run and not weary and they shall walk and not tired."

Eagle's characteristics are so desirable that God presents them as examples to us to emulate in order to renew our strength.

To renew strength is to be refreshed, to improve in knowledge or to be equipped with new energy to carry out required tasks. Eagles in their old age still operate with the same strength and capacity because of its renewing habit.

The eagle renews its strength by deliberately removing its old feathers that impair its activeness. And it waits while it grows the new feathers.

Anyone who has the eagles renewing habit will run without being weary mentally even at old age. Moses was 120 years when he passed the leadership instructions and baton to Joshua. Everything that Joshua achieved as a successful leader was based on the leadership manual that Moses gave to him.

Moses' great leadership knowledge can be traced to his learning. Outside the fact that he grew up in Pharaoh's palace where important decisions were made, he was nowhere near a perfect leader until Jethro his father in-law taught him some aspects of leadership. In Exodus Chapter 18, we have the account that Moses did not shove off Jethro's counsel but acted accordingly because, he understood that no one has the monopoly of wisdom. Imagine a man like Moses having had numerous encounters with God, sitting while Jethro tutored him on leadership? A delusional leader who lives in his own reality will never learn from others. He would prefer to wallow in his ignorance. Every good leader must be flexible to learn in order to keep pace with global developments.

Lee Kuan Yew, former Singapore minister, a graduate of London school of economics became Singapore Prime Minister at the age of 35 and transformed Singapore from a very poor nation to a world economic giant. Jose Mujica, former president of Uruguay was 75 years old when he became the president. He left office in 2015 leaving the country in a very healthy economical state. Joash was seven years when he became king in Israel. He was successful all the days that he had priest Jehoiada tutoring him.

Paul Kagame, the president of Rwanda became democratically elected president at the age of 42. He stabilized the country that was ravaged by many years of war, the war that led to the genocide that claimed approximately one million lives in 100 days. Today, the country is one of the fastest growing economies in Africa. The country is so peaceful that Paul Kagame strolls on the streets with his wife without security agents around them.

Former Chinese leader (Deng), one of those who started the economic revolution that the Chinese are enjoying today said, "I don't care whether the cat is white or black, it's a good cat as long as it catches mice."

We might be fighting the wrong battle if all we are after is having youthful leaders because that has not really been the challenge, the challenge has been the lack of leaders with sound judgments and the will to do the right thing.

Chapter Seven
REPAIRING THE BROKEN BRIDGE

Every society and race have their struggles and ugly side. If you have related with people closely, you might have met good as well as bad people from every color, race and religion because evil has no special color, race or religion.

Stereotyping people has never built any relationship bridge, rather it has produced hate and crises in every corner of human existence.

The politicians are united without barriers, they sit and dine together, but have done well in dividing the uninformed masses to war among themselves. These are oxen carrying the arks, and as long as we allow them to keep our heads under the waters, the bridge of love, unity and progress will not be built in our society.

Long before religion came to Africa's shore, we were guided by morality and conscience. Disputes were resolved based on morality. Back in the days in African history, when one is found stealing, kidnapping, or in a premeditated murder, ether by physical attack or diabolical means, such a person would either be killed or banished from the community. These acts were based on justice and morality, which is the core believes of every religion.

If such was our culture and value, how did Africa get to this point where killing each other has become a norm? I suppose your guess would be as good as mine!

When we have religious leaders teaching us to put religion over relationships and national interest, religion over love and peace, our unity and coexistence will be threatened.

Anyone who preaches violence, or hate against any group or persons base on their religious believes or on the guise of national interest is an enemy to humanity irrespective of his or her religious affiliation or ethnicity.

National interest!

Any country with multiple religious faces must take off any religious form and put nation building and growth first. Many African and 3rd world countries are religiously overzealous, and some of our leaders capitalize on that to satisfy us religiously. No wealthy nation or western country spends national wealth sending citizens for religious pilgrimages on yearly bases like Africans do. And bad enough, all the nations that engage in these practices have the same crises.

When a nation chooses religious knowledge over innovation and information, they will breed extremists and terrorists rather than development.

True God is found in the hearts of those who love justice. And it is unjust when we put religion above our national interest.

In Jeremiah 29:7 the Bible says, "Seek the peace of the city where I have caused you to be carried away captives, and pray unto the Lord for it, for in her peace shall you have peace."

There's a law of give and take. What you give is what you get in return. If you want a peaceful environment where people can prosper, create it. God in His wisdom commanded the Jews to pray for the peace of Babylon where they were strangers as captives. The Babylonians destroyed the land of Israel. Israel would have seen them as their enemies but God said no, pray for the peace of the land for your own sake.

So it is an unpardonable sin for anyone to groom citizens in the name of religion and turn them against their own country.

We learn religion and forget our history, thereby building a nation without a reference point. History gives us understanding of where we are coming from, where we have failed and where we must improve on.

From my Christian understanding, "We don't learn religion but we learn the life of Christ that is embedded in love. A life based on equality, justice, tolerance and sacrifice." And such is not learned in any secular place of study because it's a life of faith in the spirit.

In all fairness, not every Muslim agrees with those that engage in the act of sending a child who has no knowledge or former education to religious schools. Any child who is only religiously indoctrinated will grow up putting his religion over his nation.

And once they come of age, and realized that their religious values have no role in the society, and that they cannot articulately convey their ideology peacefully, they will try to enforce it with arms.

People are attracted to light, if our practice is pure, people will be attracted to it. God is not weak to be defended with bows.

Your love for God is expressed by how much love and service you render to humanity. Any exercise in God's name that is void of sacrifice and services to humanity is a religious exercise in futility.

Love and compassion without boundaries remain the greatest gospel any leader can preach. When you apply these tools, it will become a bridge that eventually wins trust and at the same time enlarge your circle.

In Luke 6:33, Jesus explains that going beyond your boundary is an example of true sacrifice. "And if you do good to those who are good to you, what credit is that to you? Even sinners do that" (NIV).

Even in our differences, we can still find a common ground to stand for our nation's interest. We are stronger together and weaker divided. Our full potential can only be harnessed when we are united with one purpose.

Chapter Eight
THE POWER OF UNITY

"…..Now nothing that they began to do will be withheld from them" (Genesis 11:1).

This was God speaking here about the power of unity. And it was the story of the migrants from the east It's about their unity, their vision, strength and achievement. They had a vision, and they understood unity and oneness of purpose, is the strength to achieve their desire. They embarked on building the famous tower of Babel.

Their attitude toward nation building and unity is something that every government and leader should desire. They were driven by foresight and they were building for generational impact.

In the above Scripture, Genesis 11 verse 1, the Bible says "The whole earth had one language and one speech."

Before you conclude that the secret of their success was because they literally spoke in one language, may I ask, even in your family, community or country where people speak a single language, how united are they to embark on building a tower that will be as high as heaven? Any project with one language and one speech with a divided mind will not thrive. One language and one speech here speak of their unity of purpose for the common good of all.

Verse (Two), "And it came to pass, as they journeyed from the east, that they found a plain in the land of Shinar, and they dwelt there. Then they said to one another, Come, let us make bricks and bake them **thoroughly**. They had brick for stone, and they had asphalt for mortar. And they said, Come, let us build ourselves a city, and a tower whose top is in the heavens; let us make a name for ourselves, lest we be scattered abroad over the face of the whole earth" Genesis 11:1-4 (NKJV).

Understand that this was after the flood that came upon the earth. So, people were trying to find settlements and balance after that devastating flood. Challenges have been part of human existence from Genesis. The state of any nation is as poor or as healthy as their leader's mindset.

The migrants from the East in the above Scripture settled in a place called Shinar. Shinar is in (Mesopotamia) and the word Mesopotamia means a (land between two rivers or a land of rivers)

When people are united with a common purpose, nothing will be impossible for them to achieve. To build their vision and the future they desired, see what they did.

"They had brick for stone" In (I Peter 2:5) the Bible says, "You yourselves like living stones are being built up as a spiritual house." Figuratively, we are the stones that must come together for our nation building.

They did not only gather the stones, they made the stones of the best quality.

In Verse three, "They said let us burn the bricks thoroughly for the structure. They understood that for any structure to stand the times, the stone must be thorough."

Things are falling apart in our society because the stones trusted for the structures are not thoroughly made for the tasks. Students are not thoroughly taught in our government colleges and universities. Our security agencies are not thoroughly prepared for the weighty task before them.

The primary aim of the men from the east in building that great tower was to create a safe and comfortable environment, and to leave a legacy for themselves. When a government thoroughly equips the people with knowledge and favorable policies, building a tower becomes easier.

Anyone in leadership that wants to achieve success must learn to carry everyone along, and in return, those carried along can help in building the nation.

We might not get every stone in perfect shape, but like the men from the east, in other for the building to stand, the stones must stay together. Not all stones come perfectly squared, some come perfect while others come with broken edges and half cuts. Yet, there's never a fight amongst the stones on who is more important, because the stone's value and beauty is only seen in the building, not in their singleness.

Perfect structures are not built with perfect bricks alone, but with imperfect bricks as well. But as a matter of necessity, the bricks must be put together by a skillful builder in order to have a perfect structure. This is why we must end the era of oxen carrying our arks in Africa.

The bricks are to be put together by skillful builders, we must find the best hands amongst us to lead… Our nation and continent's building should be paramount; and we are that living stone that must be united if we are to build it.

The attitude of the men from the east as recorded in Genesis 11 is a complete epitome of patriotism. Their visions were (1) to build a city, (2) to build a tower, (3) to make a good name, (4) so they don't scatter abroad on the face of the earth.

The core vision of every good leader should be based on these, "to unite the people and engage in building their cities and nation. The migrants were to build a city to live together. Every leader in their various capacities, from local to national level should make building their cities a priority. To build a city is a primary debt every leader owes to the citizens. It speaks of providing a comfortable living environment. After building a city, the next agenda should be to build a tower.

Building a Tower

The Chinese seems to have better understanding of "building a tower and making a name lest we be scattered abroad". In times past, the Chinese were scattered all over the world as cheap laborers. Over time, Chinese leaders selflessly provided an environment for the citizens that were once scattered abroad as cheap laborers to return and invest. Now, every Chinese community has a production factory. They returned not as cheap laborers but as directors and employers of labor. Jesus said, "The children of this world are in their generation wiser than the children of light" (Luke 16:8). Building a city without a tower is like a temporal stimulus package.

This is the much many leaders have achieved. They built beautiful cities for living but nothing to engage the dwellers with. Despite the large Chinese population (about twice America's population), the crime rate in America is more than that of China because most Chinese are engaged while many Americans are not. Other countries like Mexico, Venezuela, Colombia, South Africa, Nigerian, El-Salvador and some other countries have an alarming crime rate far more than China. Any beautiful city without a tower to engage the people will engage in the battles that idleness produces, and like the common phrase goes, "an idle heart is the devil's workshop."

What the men from the east built wasn't just a literal structure like skyscraper or a monument. This is because, no man can literarily build anything that will reach the heavens. Monuments and skyscrapers don't keep people together but building a sustainable structure where people can benefit and live off will keep them working.

During the Soviet era under Nikita Khrushchev, the Soviet Union sent their scientists to the space to flex their might. This became a challenge to their rival, namely the American government. On May 5th 1961, under John F. Kennedy Americans launched into space to show the Soviets that what they can do, Americans can do. Several other nations have gone to the space and some have gone multiple times since then. In 2003, the Chinese made their first space trip. And not too long after that, they were ready to start mining the mineral they discovered in space, making them the first country to embark on space mineral exploration.

While the rest were making their expensive space trips a military and power affairs, the Chinese space vision was on business and profit affairs. When you have a tower building vision, your thought pattern will be different. And your people cannot scatter abroad because each will be engaged, contributing their share- 'employment.' Tower builders engage in an endless research for national and human development. In a nutshell, let us build a tower that we may not scatter abroad "create a working or an industrial environment so that none of us will migrate elsewhere in search of a means of surviving." The reason Africans are scattered abroad as destitute on the face of the earth is because their leaders have no tower -building -mentality.

America, China and other world powers are strong today because of their undeniable presence in many parts of the world.

The first Apostles that Jesus called, Peter, Andrew, James and John understood the essence of team work. This explains why Jesus conferred more with them- "Peter, James and John" while He was doing His earthly ministry. These men were fishermen by trade and supported each other in their businesses.

The lesson here is to understand that with unity everything is possible. If we can tap into each other's strength, the work would be easier. We have witnessed a more divisive Nigeria under President Buhari, the exact scenario in America under President Trump who all his time in office built walls of division.

I believe there are potentials in every region for the enhancement of our nation, and failing to carry every region along is tantamount to failure in leadership. Politics is a game but leadership is a call. When you bring political games into leadership you end up encouraging a vendetta at the expense of the nation.

Despite the struggles in every sphere under Buhari's administration, history would have been kind to him if he had exercised inclusiveness in his government. But as things are, he will definitely be leaving office with Nigeria being more divided and impoverished than he met her, and a lesson for our future leaders not to follow. They must build the bridge to the East, West, North and South for a better Nigeria that we may not scatter broad as destitute anymore.

Chapter Nine
BRIDGE THE GAP BY INNOVATION

To bridge a gap is to connect two things or to make the difference between them smaller. The politicians are untouchable even in their brutal and unaccountable leadership because they have the means of manipulation. When a country is run mostly by government managed resources, the citizens are impoverished while the officials are enriched. But when the citizens are empowered having control of the economy through entrepreneurship, the state or nation gets rich through the tax payers returns. With this, there will be balance and the gap between the high and low will be minimal, and the political office will be less attractive. No country is rich until that wealth reflects in the lives of her citizens.

Any country where politicians control the wealth is a nation without headway. Why wouldn't the citizens be afraid of a man with wealth and political power to sign laws? One of the reasons we have some security agencies in frequent corruption and extortion is because they are under paid by politicians.

In my reasoning, it is illogical for any politician who daily sits comfortably in his well-furnished air-conditioned office to earn more than a lecturer in the classroom, a security agent on the highway or at the border, or a doctor in the theatre room etc. African politicians control the wealth and resources of the land, they sell to over pay themselves and give crumps to the true laborers of the land.

Dangers of total reliance on natural resource

Now, let me outline few among many risks when countries rely only on mineral resource as a means of sustainability. When it comes to business relationship or national and human development, anyone that offers anything that adds value to that effect must be welcomed with an open arm if the terms are favorable and well spelt.

Some Arabian countries have done well in managing their oil and gas unlike Nigeria that has for years abused her wealthy resources through corruption. And in retrospect, what was supposed to be a blessing has been overturned. Sometime in 2009, an Australian friend handed me a magazine published in Cambodia. At the time the magazine was published, Cambodia had discovered their oil and gas, and the government was skeptical in diving into exploration of the oil. They have seen the negative side of depending solely on oil in some countries and they were careful not to make the same mistake. In the said magazine, the author cited the negative effect of Nigeria's dependency on oil saying, "Cambodia should be careful so that their oil will not become a curse like Nigeria's oil has become a curse to Nigeria due to corruption and mismanagement".

This reality and ugly example saddened my heart for a moment, and with her soft Australian accent she said to me, "Andrew, that's heartbreaking, isn't it?

While it is understood that Nigeria's case is largely due to mismanagement and corruption, it's also important to understand that no tree grows tall unless it spreads its roots downward.

For any nation to solely depend on oil as the only means of revenue is like one hanging his treasure box on a leaf. 95% of the countries that depends on oil are not the same that determine the price. Having weighed all that transpired between Obama's administration and Russia under Putin's administration, I can tell you how risky it is for any nation to rely on oil as her only means for survival.

Obama, Putin's face-off!

I strongly believe that the crash in oil price in 2015 was deliberate, and an effort to weaken Russia by Obama's administration. Among others, Russia largely depends on oil and military hardware exports to run their economy. While crude is freely traded in the world market, hardware's are not due to the United Nations Arms control Treaty that doesn't allow any nation to trade arms at will.

So, Russia's dependence on crude at the time was high and at the same time, the price was at its peak and like other (OPEC) Countries, Russia's economy was doing relatively good. In Putin's characteristics zeal to show his muscle, he went to Syria in support of Bashar al-Assad's regime that American government was trying to oust by empowering the opposition against the ruling government.

After series of unheeded warnings for Russia to withdraw its support for Assad's regime, America had no other choice than to crash the oil price which Russia largely depended on to run their economy and military. Not too long after the crash of oil price, Russia's military presence in Syria gradually diminished because you need inflow of cash to engage in bombings. When this happened, in order to be the only power broker in the oil market, America for the first time in 40 years released their oil into the market selling at their own pegged price without OPEC's consent. This action handicapped other (OPEC) members as they had no other choice than to sell at American fixed rate or keep their oil and starve. The crash gravely affected countries like Nigeria that solely relied on oil. Our faith should not be anchored on something that is under the control of others.

Our positive transformation is not on oil, and if we must rise to have our say as an independent nation, we must shift our reliance on what the world powers controls. The only way any country can escape being a puppet in the hands of the heavy weight countries is to shift her dependency from an item it can easily be manipulated with and move to innovation.

The greatest asset any nation can pride in is its human capital. If a nation lacks good heads to manage resources, the land will be poor amidst her diamond fields and oil wells.

Super power space is not a right given to any nation, it is a space that countries take by economic strength or by military might. Innovation and industrialization gave China their space among the super powers. Nigeria has the potential if it can be harnessed. The government must create a safe working and market-based environment, and also empower her citizen's innovatively. I don't want to use China's economic growth in comparison with that of UK or U.S. because many would think the edge is due to their large population. But for the sake of information, China's economic growth in 2016 was 6.7% against America's 1.6%. And the trend of that growth gap still remains till date. But let's narrow it and compare UK's economic growth with that of Taiwan. The UK with over 65 million population based on 2016 report recorded 1.8% economic growth, whereas Taiwan with 23.4 million populations based on 2016 report recorded 2.6% economic growth in the same year. And the trend still remains to this year 2022

Africa, especially Nigeria at this stage must explore other options, like China and other fast-growing economic powers, and any nation that can offer that partnership should be embraced with an open arm. The fact that some Arabian countries have done well in providing the basic needs for their citizens, and accumulated some sizeable wealth for the future.

On this note, I must commend UAE's leadership and vision in making Dubai such a beauty and attraction. But in terms of technology, Arabs are not topnotch in 21st century advance technology. And like other African countries they depend largely on oil. But what happens when or if oil fails like in Nigeria and Venezuela where oil cash is currently not reflecting in the countries experience? It is high time every visionary leader comes to term with the reality that for our nations to survive, it must shift its dependency on oil to other innovative discoveries.

Israel and her Arab Neighbors

Let's bring Israel and her Arab neighbors into this equation to see how Africa can benefit from both parties in Nation building. Israel is a secular state not a religious state. They attack you only when you physically attack their nation. Unlike the Arabs, they attack you when they feel religiously and nationally attacked. Israel's driving force is what adds value to their economy. Whereas most Arabs go after what adds value to their religion because they have no need for industrial development hence their oil can still flow in the world market. As much as relationships must be maintained on both sides, Nigeria has reasons to push for stronger bilateral ties with Israel for obvious reasons. The Jews are among the best scientists in the world. The Jews agricultural production technic is topnotch in the world. The Jews are connected to major discoveries that are piloting affairs of civilization and modernization. Although it is not the biggest nation in the region, they have the strongest military arsenal in the region. And they have been able to sustain this and maintain a stable economy which is not dependent on oil but through innovation. The greatest wealth is not deposited in the soil but in humans. Every expensive product you buy is expensive not mainly because of the product but because of the brain behind it. So, knowledge is the most expensive commodity and that's why there's a saying that, "knowledge is power".

The nations that invested in human development are those ruling the world and they will continue to do so without a doubt. The reason for this little analysis between the Arabs and their Israeli neighbors is for elaboration and objectivity.

Mineral resources are meant to be harnessed and the proceeds used in developing the human force that will drive the affairs through innovation.

Having explained this, it is important that Nigeria and other oil producing nations rely less on oil and more on human capital through innovation. In 2017, at a time when Nigeria was in great financial distress, oil price was down, the opportunity to get refocused was presented to Nigeria at the (Africa - Israelis business submits), but Nigeria missed out. They missed out not because the leaders were not aware of it; they missed out because the president (like the biblical ox) called back the Nigerian delegates simply because Benjamin Netanyahu Israel's Prime Minister was to address the conference. Nigeria missed out because of Buhari's rigid and retrogressive state of mind that has taken the country back by several years.

There's no government or investor who doesn't know the great potentials in Nigeria. But these potentials are not harnessed because the environment, mostly under Buhari's government is not favorable. All the challenges facing Nigeria today, from insecurity, infrastructure and building a strong economy through innovation are what Israel is known for. The chance to relate and learn what would have probably become a game changer was missed.

My emphasis here is not putting a country over another or preferring one over the other, but it is about putting the interest of our nation over religion and personal fascism. Without prejudice, Africa needs that hidden Western pearl that makes them what they are, and a safe haven for Africans escaping the harshness of another continent.

CHAPTER TEN
HISTORY AND LESSON TO LEARN

In Nigeria's history, it is true that the country has engaged in a civil war that shouldn't have happened. The civil war of 1967-1970 was not the only war Nigerians knew. As a major player in West African affairs, every outbreak of conflict within the region throws invitation for Nigeria's intervention. The most notable war was between Liberia and Sierra Leone from 1991 to 2002. With Nigeria's involvement overseas and experience at home, what lessons have we learned? They say "those who fail to learn from the past will live to repeat the same mistake."

A little synopsis of Nigeria's history, Liberia, and Sierra Leone's civil war and the lessons to learn!

Sometime in 1960, 'Sir Ahmadu Bello' Premier of the Northern region of Nigeria was granted an interview on BBC. In his interview, he said he would northernize the labor force in his region, thereby depriving other regions from civil work in the north. He was very particular and critical about the Igbo's domineering attitude. He further noted that on the grounds that there's no qualified Northerner, he would hire a foreign expatriate or other Nigerian tribes on contract basis.

Sir Ahmadu Bello spoke from a very conservative perspective of life. This unconventional statement from Sir Ahmadu Bello was backed by Samuel Ladoke Akintola, the Premier of Western Nigeria. Akintola's stand on Bello's decision contradicted his person, as a known activist who fought for people's right to live freely. This did not sit well among the Easterners who were scattered all over Nigeria in their adventurous characteristic. With such a statement, the military high ranked mainly of the East and Southern extraction felt that the unity and coexistent of Nigeria was under threat. And in the most obnoxious manner, decided to eliminate the arrow heads of those deem to pose threats to the one - Nigeria course.

In my quest to pass liable information to my readers, I did my research on Nigeria's history and the roles of our founding fathers in imparting us today. In my findings, Nnamdi Azikiwe and Obafemi Awolowo are the few that did good service to Nigeria as a country. Nnamdi Azikiwe in particular was one man who wholly put Nigeria first before tribe.

This is probably why history is out of Nigeria's curriculum because you cannot talk history without exposing the acts of the history makers.

They know that most of those we celebrate and hail as heroes sowed the seed of discord that is plaguing Nigeria today.

This is not an inditement against anyone, or a justification of the military action that happened, but a critical look at what resulted in the military interference of 1966 multiple assassinations of political leaders. The military was not satisfied with the handling of the perceived Igbo dominance, and in reality, the handling lacked leadership wisdom.

(1) If there was a domination of the Easterners in the Northern and Western region, such hate speech from a Northern leader and a Western leader was not needed to remedy the situation. There's nowhere in the world where hate speech has brought a peaceful resolution to matters.

(2) In business and trade, no region should feel insecure about the Easterners dominance because it is like a divine gift to them, and they've mastered the trade skills.

But for them to also dominate in government agencies in other regions was an administrative lapse. Even though it is constitutionally right for anyone to work anywhere, it is ethically unacceptable. This is the very scenario under Buhari's administration, where one region has dominated almost every aspect. If it was wrong then for one group to dominate, it is wrong now.

(3) The situation should have been handled in a more civilized manner by the aggrieved regions so that their counterpart wouldn't feel sidelined or marginalized. It should have been a duty call for regional leaders to make adjustments where needed than for the military involvement that happened.

Military interferences in civil affairs in Africa have done more harm than good on the continent. For the Nigerian military to have stepped into a matter of governance was not helpful, and such is still the order of the day, where armed forces are used to intimidate and silence the voice of the masses. Administrative adjustments should have been made where qualified indigenes are considered first, and in areas where they are not available, qualified persons from other regions can fill the space.

When you choose violence over dialogue or discrimination in tackling administrative dysfunction, you become obnoxious to the subjects. Eastern leaders should have called other leaders to discuss the danger of such hate and discriminatory approach, and as policy, propose national rules guiding choice of labor force and appointment positions that presents a balance or show federal character.

The actions from these supposedly heroes are the reasons we are here today as a disunited nation. Reading the history of what transpired, you will arrive at the conclusion that the action or approach lacked any sense of good judgement or diplomacy.

You may not share my views on this, and yes, you have the right to your opinion. When we profess in our anthem that "the labors of our heroes past shall not be in vain," sometimes I ask 'what brilliant achievement for the good of Nigeria should some of them be rewarded for?'

Truly, freedom is good. It is the fundamental right of everyone. Until you are freed everything you have can be a mere fiasco. Nothing equals the price for freedom, it is the most priceless gift that God desires everyone to enjoy because it gives you the right of choice. But for most Africans and third world countries, we are still hoping that our freedom would come soon. For now, what we have is an exchange from the hands of meek and lenient European colonial masters to the hands of oppressive leaders who have enslaved their people.

Most of those we honor as heroes particularly in Nigeria are those who sowed the seeds of discord. I am not personally proud to call them heroes!

Signs & Lessons from Sierra Leone

A man by name Joseph Saidu Momoh served as President of Sierra Leone from November 28, 1985 to April 29, 1992. A professional soldier drawn into politics, Momoh rose from the enlisted ranks to the highest position of (Major-General) in the Sierra Leone Military Forces.

In 1985 Momoh succeeded President Siaka Stevens by becoming the only candidate in a one-party election in the form of a referendum under the banner of the All People's Congress (APC).

Momoh declared a state of economic emergency early in his rule, granting himself greater control over Sierra Leone's economy, but he was not regarded as a dictator. Instead, his people viewed him as far too weak and inattentive to the affairs of the state, allowing his notoriously corrupt advisors to manipulate matters behind the scenes. Sierra Leone's economy gradually disintegrated under Momoh's rule, and the country's currency decreased in value. Sierra Leone reached the point under President Momoh where it could no longer afford to supply gas and electricity to the country.

What a coincidence that President Buhari and President Momoh have perfect similarities. More striking is that the acronym of both political parties is the same. We, however, hope and pray not to have the war experience that happened in Sierra Leone while the APC regime remains.

Chapter Eleven
HOW JESUS DEALT WITH CORRUPTION

The all-knowing God knew the harm bribing and corruption would cause in a nation, He forewarned Israel against bribes right after they departed Egypt.

In Exodus 23:8 the Bible says, "Do not accept a bribe, for a bribe blinds those who see and twists the words of the innocent" (NIV).

All through the Old Testament, there was contention between the prophets of God and corrupt officials. Their fight against corrupt leaders earned them persecution, and imprisonment as it is today.

Prophet Isaiah speaking against their corrupt practices says in Isaiah 1:23, "Your rulers are rebels and companions of thieves; everyone loves a bribe and chases after rewards. They do not defend the orphan, nor does the widow's plea come before them."

In Ecclesiastes 7:7 the Bible says, "For oppression makes a wise man mad, and a bribe corrupts the heart"

Corruption and oppression are twin brothers. Every corrupt leader is also oppressive and every oppressive leader is corrupt. From the Scripture above, you cannot be a wise man and endure being perpetually oppressed by corrupt leaders.

In Proverbs 17:23 it says, "A wicked man receives a bribe from the bosom to pervert the ways of justice" (KJV).

Time and again, God warned Israel against bribery and corrupt practice because where such evil thrives, justice is absent. Israel's leadership unwilling heart to change from those evil practices resulted in the nation's ill fate as it were.

Little wonder the Bible says, "By justice a king gives country stability, but those who are greedy for bribes tear it down" Proverbs 29:4 (NIV).

Without a doubt, this is one major problem confronting Africa and many other third world countries, where their leaders pervert justice for gain.

Men like trees

"And he looked up, and said, I see men like trees, walking" (Mark 8: 24). The story of the blind man is a familiar story. He was brought to Jesus to be healed of his blindness, after Jesus touched his eyes, He asked him what he saw. In response, the man said he saw men like trees walking. The man was not wrong with what he said, because what he saw was what he said. The only problem was that, the man was seeing beyond the natural at the time. If your eyes are opened to see what happens in the spiritual realm, you would indeed agree that life is far beyond what you see naturally. Jesus did not want him to perpetual remain in that state of seeing only spiritually, because he wouldn't have been able to relate with natural men while in that state, so Jesus touched him again so he could see like natural men do.

"Now let me sing to my Well-beloved a song of my beloved regarding His vineyard:

My Well-beloved has a vineyard on a very fruitful hill. He dug it up and cleared out its stones, and planted it with the choicest vine. He built a tower in its midst, and also made a winepress in it; so He expected it to bring forth good grapes, But it brought forth wild grapes. "And now, O inhabitants of Jerusalem and men of Judah, Judge, please, between Me and my vineyard. What more could have been done to my vineyard

That I have not done in it? Why then, when I expected it to bring forth good grapes, did it bring forth wild grapes? And now, please let Me tell you what I will do to My vineyard: I will take away its hedge, and it shall be burned; And break down its wall, and it shall be trampled down. I will lay it waste; it shall not be pruned or dug, but there shall come up briers and thorns. I will also command the clouds that they rain no rain on it. For the vineyard of the Lord of hosts is the house of Israel,

And the men of Judah are His pleasant plant. He looked for justice, but behold, oppression; For righteousness, but behold, a cry for help" Isaiah 5:1-7 (NKJV).

Depending on one's displayed character, humans are often likened with animals like "lion, hose, sheep, goat, fox, dog, eagle, snake and so on." In Nigeria for example, people of exceptional characters are often referred to as Iroko trees. Similarly, humans are Biblically likened to certain trees like "palm tree, olive tree, cedar tree, fig tree, vine, bramble" and so on.

For example, in the Book of Revelation Chapter 11 verse 3 to 5 and verse 10, the Bible speaking of God's two witnesses for His end time mission referred to them as Olive trees. He referred to them as olive tree because olive stands for anointing, and these men will come with uncommon prophetic anointing to fulfill Gods end time mandate.

When Jotham stood on mount Gerizim to cry against the people of Shechem in Judges Chapter 9 Verses 7-15, he used trees in his case against the people of Shechem.

One peculiar phrase that was used by the Hutu's to provoke the Rwandan genocide against the Tutsis was "Cut down the tall trees." The Tutsi tribe were described or called "the tall trees." Even those possessed by demon spirits to perpetuate evil still understood that humans are likened to trees.

However, for the purpose of the subject matter, I will be using palm trees and fig trees. Each of these trees has their special characteristics and why humans are likened to them.

In Psalm 92:12-14 the Bible says, "The righteous shall flourish like a palm tree, He shall grow like a cedar in Lebanon. Those who are planted in the house of the Lord Shall flourish in the courts of our God. They shall still bear fruit in old age; they shall be fresh and flourishing."

There're different types of palm trees, namely "The Palmyra palm; Date palm; Elaeis guineensis palm; Nipa palm; Sugar palm; and the Coconut palm."

Being a Nigerian, I would write from the context of the palm tree that is commonly found in our communities and that is the "Elaeis guineensis palm tree" and how it relates to this topic.

Olive represents our spirituality, spiritual authority and total spiritual wellness. The Fig represents our physical wellness and total comfort. And the Palm tree speaks of our character, integrity, growth and fruitfulness.

These three trees are typical expression of how God designed life to be. That is (one) to have a sound spiritual life, (two) a sound physical life, and (three) to be in right standing and to be fruitful.

The above Scripture psalm 92 says, "The 'righteous' shall flourish like a palm tree."

The word 'righteous' "is to be characterized by uprightness, morality, justifiable or virtuous."

In other words, for someone to be considered a right man, he must be upright just like a palm tree that naturally grows in uprightness. Uprightness is the key to good leadership or stewardship. An upright man doesn't play partial. He could be a career politician but will never play politics in leadership. When a leader is upright, he is productive in every aspect of his leadership actions, just like every aspect of a palm tree is needful.

For being a right or an upright leader, you are rewarded in return with support by your subjects to see your success in everything. And that is the stage where leaders flourish. There's no flourishing until there's uprightness because your flourishing comes by being able to fully tap into the hidden strength of everything within your amour.

From a palm tree many kinds of oil are extracted… Wine is extracted and sugar is produced, from the leaves, weaving is made for shelter, and broom is made for sweeping. Yes, every person has need of a sweeping broom to sweep off anything that wants to defy his character and decency.

Palm tree fronds are always green. When a frond of a palm tree changes its color, it becomes brown. This change is a sign of dryness or deadness on that frond. Palm trees do not revive or hold on to any dying fronds. What happens next is that, the brownish frond is detached from the palm and it falls off.

No upright or right person associates with any frond with negative color, or anyone that misrepresents his good image. Any government or leader that has unproductive people or persons and fails to cut such persons off, is unproductive also. When a leader claims to be at war against corruption and yet has notorious corrupt officials in his cabinet, it shows that the leader is hypocritical boss of corruption.

These are not man's fabricated words but the characteristics of a palm tree that an upright man should possess.

Another great quality of a palm tree is that it cannot be grafted. This nature of the palm speaks of its genuineness, originality and uniqueness. Upright people would rather stand-alone like the palm tree than to compromise their integrity. Uprightness requires that your name is not used to plant people in places they are not qualified to be. Palm trees only grow from its seed, not by grafting. Right people are not doubled faced, they're original in their color and productive in their words and actions.

Palm trees are not affected by drought because they have the ability to locate waters downward. A right leader should have foresight and the ability to provide sustainable ideas as a justification for his position.

I could go on and on talking about qualities of a palm tree- its fruit and the numerous oils it provides and why the Bible likens the righteous to it. I pray that God will raise us, individuals with palm tree qualities to take over the leaderships of our nations.

Men and fig relationship

There're numerous trees that are much larger and taller than the fig tree. But the tall and giant trees don't have the natural qualities of a fig tree. Most giant trees don't bear edible fruits, the few that do, like African breadfruit tree, has its dangers. For example, during the storm they don't offer safety. Giant trees are mostly used for timber. Timbers are likened to individuals who through their own schemes build or grow their own empires. Timbers are private merchandizing commodities. That is why some rich individuals are referred to as "men of timber and caliber" because they stand-out.

We all know how dangerous timber can be if it falls. Throughout the Bible, Jesus never used giant trees when referring to people because He didn't want us to rely on what could kill when it falls. Also, men are supposed to freely relate with each other, and not meant to be out of reach by others. A little olive tree in relationship with others is more valuable in God's perspective than out of reach giant trees. Life should be all about service, serving God and serving people. This explains why Jesus always uses fruitful trees that men could relate with in His illustrations.

That is what Jesus represents and looks out for, He came in the form of man so that He could relate with men, in order to impart men with His life for the purpose of imparting others.

Chapter Twelve
THE FIG TREE

The relationship between Figs and humans is something worth studying. Amongst other trees, the fig tree is the oldest recorded in the Bible. It is dated way back to when Adam was in the Garden of Eden.

In Genesis 3:7 the Bible says, "Then the eyes of both of them were opened, and they knew that they were naked; and they sewed fig leaves together and made themselves coverings."

Over the years from the very beginning of time, men developed the warm relationship with the fig tree and trusted its remedy so greatly.

The fig was there as a temporal covering when Adam fell. When Israel left the land of bondage Egypt, Joshua, Caleb and ten others went as spies in preparation for taking the Promised Land. On their return, they brought fig fruits, (Numbers 13: 23). The fig was there for Hezekiah's cure as recommended by the Prophet in (Isaiah 38:21). It was there as food for David and his armies when Abigail provided it to atone for her household in (I Samuel 25:18). The fig tree offering itself as a temporal covering in the garden was an access to gain that trust that men eventually placed on it. And being there at Israel's critical period of taking the Promised Land was strategic, in continuation to its services to men.

Fig has rich nutrients that are very vital for our wellbeing like "vitamin A, vitamin B1, vitamin B2, calcium, iron, phosphorus, manganese, sodium, potassium, chlorine and many more."

This richness is deliberately and divinely deposited to answer to the needs of men.

But "The next day, when they had come out from Bethany, He was hungry. And seeing from afar a fig tree having leaves, He went to see if perhaps He would find something on it. When He came to it, He found nothing but leaves, for it was not the season for figs. In response Jesus said to it, "Let no one eat fruit from you ever again" Mark 11:12-14 (NKJV).

How could the fig have come this far with us from Genesis, only to fail at the last hour and in what would have been its greatest service or assignment?

Anyone who was part of our struggles, who cried when we cried, protested against injustice when we did, and eventually earned our trust for leadership only to starve us while he eats and grows fat is the corrupt fig Jesus cursed.

Adams covering with the leaves in the garden, the fig at the entrance of Israel's journey from Egypt to the Promised Land, Abigail's fig cake for David and figs cure for Hezekiah ailment were shadows of the better things to come, (the blessings we have in Christ Jesus).

Adams covering with the fig leaves after he sinned is the righteousness of Christ that covers our shortcomings, the fig in the Promised Land is our Tree of Life as we are restored in Christ to our Eden, the fig cake is a symbol of Christ being the Bread of life, and Hezekiah's fig cure is a symbol of Christ being our healer and deliverer. These were the temporal services the fig rendered to men. When Jesus was entering Jerusalem where He was to deliver humanity from temporal cure to perpetual victory, the fig was not there to help Him fulfill that mandate. The fig tree failed to produce its expected fruit.

Here's what seems like a controversy because the Bible says in that scripture, (Mark 11:13), it was not its season.

(1) I don't believe that this story would take such a large space in the Bible if it was limited to a tree not bearing fruit because it was not its season.

(2) As you would probably be pondering over this fig topic, you must understand that the person involved in this story is Jesus Christ, who was 100 percent human, and 100 percent God while on earth.

(3) It is completely impossible for Jesus not to have known that it wasn't figs season.

(4) Jesus wouldn't go to the fig tree if He was not expecting fruit from it.

The fig was seen with leaves, the fig was nourished and outstanding that it could be identified amongst other trees from afar, the potential for fruitfulness was there but it didn't produce.

The fig's many years of standing shoulder to shoulder with men in times of struggles brought it to that path of Jesus, for what would have been its ultimate service to humanity but the fig failed.

Going by the rich content and qualities of fig trees, men would hold on to it even when it is no longer productive. All through the years, people had depended on fig, with time came when it was no longer productive.

And Jesus cursing the fig is a way of telling us that we cannot continue to depend on something that cannot guaranty our wellbeing. Jesus was telling us about the shift, that the era of recycling unproductive old systems of leadership, who looks very green but don't feed the needs of the people had passed. And He is telling us that any entity or institution that is not providing a permanent cure to this plague of poverty, corruption, insecurity and underdevelopment should be discarded.

This is the picture of those with beautiful colors of the past, promising much to make people rely on them but fail at the critical stage. As time progresses what used to be helpful 100 or 50 years ago might not be relevant for today's needs. The fig had been there all through but when duty called for a paradigm shift, the fig failed because it did not understand seasons.

The fig is the picture of those who love to make their voices heard when they have nothing relevant to contribute. The pictures of those who love front position even when they have no fresh content.

The righteous or right people serve without being loud. The palm tree was not lousy but its service was eminent even at that triumphant entry of Jesus into Jerusalem. While the fig failed, palm leaves were available for Jesus to walk on into the city, John 12:13.

The cursing of the fig can also be likened to a change of system. Prior to this time in Israel's history, it was right to practice the law and get justified. But with Jesus' entrance into Jerusalem and His sacrifice for salvation, justification became obtainable only by faith in Him.

Africa is at the position where it is today because we have leaders who do not want to transit from an old system.

This is peculiar with many countries, even America where some elements refuse to let go of what they deem as white supremacists as manifested under Trumps presidency. North Korea is a concern because their leaders refuse to let go of their old systems and tradition. Russia is at odd with the West because Russian leadership refused to accept that the Soviet era has passed. The jihadists are at war with the rest of world because they refused to eradicate their old ideology of bloody or forceful conquest.

Chapter Thirteen
DEALING WITH THE FIGS!

Fig is metaphorically a system or an institution. In effecting a positive change or transformation, the hardest thing is dealing with the system that created the negative narrative. It is the hardest because every bad government that impoverishes the citizens always has few beneficiaries of that bad system.

Not only will you contend with the figs/leaders, you will also be in contention with their machinery- subjects who have subscribed to their ideologies.

Figs characterize unfruitful leaders that always capitalize on their past glory, 'I am the best type that would rather die than leave the scene.' The fig thought the cure for human predicament lies within it alone. Before Jesus' triumphant entry into Jerusalem where He eternally obtained salvation for humanity, He cursed the fig to wither. If Africa, Nigeria in particular, must see a permanent solution to her challenges, unfruitful figs in every sphere of leadership must wither. And to curse them to wither, we must also do it in Christ' way by using our voices.

In bringing sinners into repentance, longsuffering is one of Jesus' attributes. But longsuffering or patience can also be exhausted. To further explain this point, let's see what happened in Luke 13:6-9. If you read this passage carefully from the first verse, you will understand that Jesus was imploring the sinners to repent or face consequent destruction. And in doing so, He once again used the fig tree as an illustration to drive home His message saying,

"A certain man had a fig tree planted in his vineyard, and he came seeking fruit on it and found none. Then he said to the keeper of his vineyard, 'Look, for three years I have come seeking fruit on this fig tree and find none. Cut it down; why does it use up the ground?' But he answered and said to him, 'Sir, let it alone this year also, until I dig around it and fertilize it. And if it bears fruit, well. But if not, after that you can cut it down" (NKJV).

We can see that Jesus in His wisdom uses parables and trees as a metaphor to convey His message. So, we can clearly see from the above scripture that fig trees as used in the bible, are not just literal trees, but people who have been planted in their various positions to serve various purposes. To serve and satisfy humanity in return for the much that has been vested in or on them.

After three years without fruit, the owner of the vineyard said, "Cut it down" but the vinedresser says, "Give it another year to prove itself." This also tells me that a 4-year term is Biblically and constitutionally acceptable to bring down any Fig (leader) that fails to produce the dividends of leadership.

Isaiah 26:10 says, "Let grace be shown to the wicked, yet he will not learn righteousness; in the land of uprightness he will deal unjustly, and will not behold the majesty of the Lord" (NKJV).

The Father said, "Look, for three years I have come seeking fruit on this fig tree and find none. Cut it down." But the Son prayed, 'Sir, let it alone this year also, until I dig around it and fertilize it. And if it bears fruit, well. But if not, after that you can cut it down.'

The Church and other religious bodies have engaged in earnest prayers for our political leaders, but it always looked like wasteful exercise because, spiritual exercises cannot reform an ox that lacks knowledge. Those who think it's their right to plant political leaders (godfathers), have in their greed and action have done more damage. We cannot be more loving than the One whose nature is love. The same planter, who is loving and longsuffering in nature, says, "Give the fig one more year, if it bears fruit it stays, if not, cut it down."

Any public servant without tangible evidence within 2 to 3 years in office will not pacify hope even when given another 50 years. You can determine a living stream by its flow.

Time has come to muster that same energy you used in planting that nonperforming and fruitless man or woman and call it enough. That's how God operates, and if you are a political godfather, you should also do the same for the prosperity of the nation.

Chapter Fourteen
NATHANIEL, INNOCENT VICTIM!

In Genesis, the fig was the first tree ever to be mentioned, and in the Book of John chapter one, the fig was the first tree to be mentioned. There're individuals in certain families, communities, cities and nations who are household names and always in the frontlines of public affairs, but those associated with such persons are not enjoying the essence of that association.

The first we heard about Jesus' disciple Andrew, he was a disciple of John the Baptist. But after John the Baptist introduced Jesus as the way, Andrew followed Jesus and went and called his brother Peter. The next person that followed Jesus was Philip and Philip went and called Nathanael. Where was Nathanael? He was under the fig tree! When Jesus saw Nathanael He said, "Behold, an Israelite indeed, in whom is no deceit!" Nathanael was an innocent victim under a rich fig. Jesus never used such words in describing any of His other disciples. Nathanael was a good and honest citizen under the shadow of the fig, and was satisfied to be under the big name, fig! Nathanael had such a great introduction yet he was so blind with the figs' empty promises that he even asked if anything good could come out of Nazareth. We have great and honest people like Nathanael in our society, but, where are they? They are under the figs with no definitive vision, surviving by the crumbs that fall from the figs table.

The next we read or found Nathanael was among the discouraged disciples after the death of Jesus. The disciples were ready to return to their fishing business rather than pursue Jesus' commission to preach the gospel. And in that depressed state Nathanael was there probably to remind his friend Philip of his saying, if anything good could come out of Nazareth.

Jesus is the game changer. In time when the fig reigned, He came and changed the narratives. It finally downed on Nathanael that the cursed figs influence and relevance was over. When the disciples started manifesting the life and the power of Jesus that they were impacted with, Nathanael was not there for those glorious moments. He missed out on Jesus' teachings and impartation because he trusted the figs' promises. Nathanael was an innocent and loyal victim of a unfruitful fig/leader.

Jonathan, unthinkable loyalist!

And Saul's son Jonathan went to David at Horesh and helped him find strength in God. "Don't be afraid," he said. "My father, Saul will not lay a hand on you. You will be king over Israel, and I will be second to you. Even my father Saul knows this." The two of them made a covenant before the Lord. Then Jonathan went home, but David remained at Horesh (I Samuel 23:16-18).

The story of Jonathan is one that each time I read it, I always have people to liken it to. I have received private messages from people telling me how bad things have become under Buhari's administration.

Yet the same people publicly support Buhari just for their temporal benefit.

Like in the case of Jonathan, he was one who knew that there was no future with his father, King Saul. He knew that the kingdom has been given to his very good friend David. But the problem with Jonathan was that, David who has the divine kingship mandate was still wandering in the wilderness. Jonathan was left with two opinions, either to leave the comfort palace of his already rejected father, or to join unsettled future king David to temporarily suffer in the wilderness.

Jonathan knew that God had given the kingdom to David, he entered a covenant with David to be part of his future cabinet when the kingdom is finally delivered into David's hands, yet Jonathan could not detach himself from the government of his father that was awaiting doom, what an irony of life.

When Donald Trump became the President of the United States of America, most Christians were excited thinking God has sent another messiah. In 2017, I was in my hotel room in Abuja during my visit to Nigeria for a church conference when God started speaking to me about Donald Trump. The message came repeatedly for about 5 to 7 times. The mind of God concerning him and his presidency was very clear to me. When different opinions were coming in the form of prophecies regarding his re-election, I never shifted from what God had said because long before Joel Biden's nomination as the Democrat's candidate, I already sent him a congratulatory message and addressed him as the next president, because God had spoken to me about it before the election.

Jonathan was aware of the divine kingdom shift from Saul to David. He knew that his father was no longer in his right senses. He should have also known that the Spirit of God had departed from Saul his father. He should have known that when light goes off darkness takes over. He should have known that the spirit of death was upon his father. When your life is ruled by sentiment you will stick around those you should have detached from. And hanging around them also may expose you to their doom.

Message to President Joe Biden

Andrew Robert
Dec 24, 2019 at 14:28

Hence we are not the author of what we dream, but God who reveals what He wants us to know, I will share what I saw.
Sometime in 2017, I saw DT, Donald Trump under pressure to leave the Whitehouse and I shared it on this platform. Today, Donald Trump is under pressure!
Again, last night I saw Trump in what seem like a rally, while he was making a speech, he fell down and was stripped naked. I saw something looking like a pile coming out of his body. He gathered himself back with the help of those around him and put on his black suit. And just then, came a noisy chant from the crowd, "Trump must go, Trump must go." And he walked towards me. And I said to him, "Mr. Trump, nobelity demands that you leave power and go.
Interpretation! Trump may resurrect from this impeachment, but he should not recontest because doing so may result in a total rejection from the Americans.

Congratulations on your election as the 46th president of America!

April 15, 2020, 07:28

To: press@joebiden.com   DETAILS

1 file 89.06 kb

Congratulations in advance to Mr. Joe Biden and to the Democrats and Americans at large!

In December 2019, in the realm of the spirit there was a shift in leadership in America. Donald Trump was rejected in the spirit realm and what that means is that, his opponent is made the next president of America.

This is purely to working of God and not man making. So here are the things we must do
(1) we must pray against any form of manipulation

must do

(1) we must pray against any form of manipulation
(2) we must pray against any form of attack on this revelation.
(3) we must pray against any form of delay to this revelation.
Attached is the snapshot of the revelation I shared on my Facebook wall in December 2019

And here are my request when the victory comes
(1) I wish to be present on your inauguration
(2) I want your government to have a good relationship with Africa, especially Nigeria
(3) Your government must uphold the Christian faith that American founding fathers laid down dearly.
Once again Congratulations!
Sincerely, Andrew Robert

--

Sent from Outlook Email App for Android

--

Sent from Outlook Email App for Android

JUNE 24, 2020

Once again, yesterday I saw a revelation. A lady walked to me and said "you told me I was going to have a baby boy, this is the boy I have him now. How did you know I would have a baby boy?" I said, it was God revealed it to me. Then she said to me, "what else did God reveal, who will be the head of custom? I said, I have not been following what's happening in your country lately, so God has not revealed to me me between the two men who will be the head. But what I can tell you is that God told me that Donald Trump is leaving office back to his house. 04:51

What God is saying about America,

June 25, 2020, 06:51

To: press

Mr. President in view,
Before your normination I sent you an email about the mind of God in the presidential race! Once again, yesterday I saw a revelation. A lady walked to me and said "you told me I was going to have a baby boy, this is the boy I have him now. How did you know I would have a baby boy?" I said, it was God revealed it to me. Then she said to me, "what else did God reveal, who will be the head of custom? I said, I have not been following what's happening in your country lately, so God has not revealed to me me between the two men who will be the head. But what I can tell you is that God told me that Donald Trump is leaving office back to his house.
I am praying for the fulfilment of what God has said concerning your presidency!
Yours sincerely
Andrew Robert

○ **Dear Mr. President,**

August 2, 2020, 05:40

To:  press   DETAILS

Congratulations once again Mr. Biden on your election in the forthcoming election. To men, the election is yet to be conducted, but in the spirit realm, the election has been concluded.
Mr. President, I want to bring your attention to the email I sent you long before you became the flag bearer of the Democrat party.
In my email, I did say that you must pray against manipulation because Donald Trump will try everything possible to manipulate the election. And I did ask you to pray against delay, as you can see it playing out now, Donald Trump is trying to delay the election and that's in other to manipulate it. Please let the Democratic party stand up and not be asleep. When God speaks the wise listens and takes action.
I pray that the will of God the Father as He has revealed it to me be done in this election and in America. And that the grace to do according to the mind of God be granted unto you.
Sincerely, Andrew Robert

Chapter Fifteen
CURE FOR THE PLAGUE

II Kings 2: 19-22 "Then the men of the city said to Elisha, "Please notice, the situation of this city is pleasant, as my lord sees; but the water is bad, and the ground barren."

And he said, "Bring me a new bowl, and put salt in it." So they brought it to him. Then he went out to the source of the water, and cast in the salt there, and said, "Thus says the Lord: 'I have healed this water; from it there shall be no more death or barrenness." So the water remains healed to this day, according to the word of Elisha which he spoke (NKJV).

To the simple, the unpleasantness was one of those things that occur in the course of life. But I will prove it that the unpleasantness in our society today is from the leadership source and if there's going to be healing in the land, we must fix it from the source.

Prophets see what ordinary people cannot see. So, Elisha knew the problem and also knew that the solution was in their hands. He asked for "a new bowl and salt." Bowl is a vessel or a container but also a spiritual metaphor. Humans are the bowl that contain the knowledge, wisdom and vision to bring cure to any unpleasant situation. Apostle Paul speaking in 2Corinthians 4:7 says, "We have this treasure in earthen vessels." The treasure needed for the cure of our insecurity, economy, infrastructures and much more.

Elisha did not just ask for a bowl but for a NEW bowl. A new bowl is a symbol of cleanness, uncorrupted or a vessel that has not yoked with dirt and corrupt status quo.

The next thing Elisha asked the people to add in the bowl was salt. Salt is a preserver. Salt produces desirable taste. Right leaders produce good and tasteful fruit. Salt is an assessable commodity in every household, the rich and the poor use it in equal share. Right leaders serve everyone and make his/her services affordable to the rich and the poor.

Jesus speaking concerning the righteous/ those standing on the right path in Matthew 5:13 says, "You are the salt of the earth." In order words, without the right people the world will be sour and tasteless.

Another important characteristic of salt that I want to share is that salt is odorless.

The odorless quality of salt is another big challenge in many countries today. It is only animals mainly among the carnivorous that attack when other animals don't smell like them. Right leaders don't discriminate; they don't play the game of nepotism and tribalism.

The genocide of Rwanda and the civil war that happened in Sierra Leone, Liberia, Nigeria and other places of the world are direct consequences of nepotism and tribalism. Today, many countries like, Nigeria are merely existing as one nation, but internally there's a tribal mistrust (smell) that has long separated them. There's so much division amongst them because of their perceived religion, and ethnic lines.

These smells are political odors created to feed their interest and the poor masses are the recipients of the aftermaths.

We have the cure

We have the cure to this plague among us. In the Garden of Eden, there was "The tree of life and there was the tree of evil and death as well." When Adam ate the tree of evil, God did not allow the corrupted Adam access to the tree of life so that he wouldn't eat and live in his corrupt state forever.

Just the same way, Jesus Christ the (Tree of Life) never gave us salvation until He defeated that tree of death, (satanic institutions). So, it translates that righteous or the right people cannot reign, work alongside evil and corrupted officials or bring justice until corrupt entities and its institutions are defeated. There must first be a cleanup of the system; get rid of the soured entities in African leadership positions, before the glory of the land can be seen.

Matthew 9:17 "Nor do they put new wine into old wineskins, or else the wineskins break, the wine is spilled, and the wineskins are ruined. But they put new wine into new wineskins, and both are preserved" (NKJV).

The system is stinking, we must open our windows to let in fresh air into our governing system. Elisha dealt with the deadly water from the source. Those who benefited from the corrupt system cannot bring the cure. It's time to bring in new bows, fresh entities with vision and love to pilot the affairs of our nations.

John Chapter 12:40 says "Lest they should see with their eyes, lest they should understand with their hearts and turn, so that I should heal them" (NKJV).

We can clearly see from the Scripture that vision and understanding precedes healing. When people are perpetually trapped in bondage it is because they are blind to the reality of life. And the reason for that is because they lack understanding.

We have the cure!

Statistics shows that Nigeria has over 2000 professional medical doctors overseas, yet Nigerian elite's travels overseas for medical attention. The same can be said of many African countries. Africa as a continent has the qualities to turn things around and give the continent a good face on the world stage. Space must be created to incorporate skillful hands home and abroad for the good of the continent. Over the years, the continent has produced great people of which many have been denied the platform to positively bring home their skill. A careful look will amaze you that some Africans in western counties have talents that could benefit the continent. But many with those talents that God brought into Africa, are living overseas because the African shore has failed to appreciate their gift due to bad leadership.

And, "the people complained against Moses, saying, "What shall we drink?" So he cried out to the Lord, and the Lord showed him a tree. When he cast it into the waters, the waters were made sweet" Exodus 15: 24-25 (NKJV).

Water here is a source of sustainability and wellness or resources. The problem here was not the absence of water or resources, but the problem was that the water was not producing the expected satisfaction it ought to. In order words, there was no proper management of the water, (resources).

We are crying that our rich minerals are not yielding the expected sweetness or benefits to the masses. And God is saying, "Throw the good trees into the (waters) to manage the nation's resources and there will be sweetness again." And remember I have established earlier that trees as used in the Bible are metaphoric words for humans.

The man God commended

As I draw the curtain to a close on this work, "when the ox carries the ark," I think it's justifiable to learn from a man who saw it all. He experienced the pinnacle of glory and the bottom side of life.

Job the man God commended!

I have established in chapter 15 "cure for the plague" and under the subtitle "we have the cure" that what is required are, recourse managers.

In Job chapter 28 verses 1-12, Job writes by the Spirit of God; Saying "Surely there is a mine for silver, and a place where gold is refined. (2) Iron is taken from the earth, and copper is smelted from the ore. (3) Man puts an end to darkness, and searches every recess for ore in the darkness and the shadow of death (4) He breaks open a shaft away from people in places forgotten by feet, they hang far away from men, they swing to and fro" (5) as for the earth, from it comes bread, but underneath it is turned up as by fire."

There's a saying that "the more you go, the more you see." There is still so much undiscovered wealth that God has deposited beneath the earth, this wealth is only at the disposal of those who dive deep into the earth. Verse 3 says, men put an end to darkness. To put an end to darkness is to cause light to shine on a thing or a place, to uncover, or to take advantage or bring into light what lies fallow. To discover, there must be a deliberate search. And to engage on a search, there must be knowledge or understanding.

In verse 5 it says, "From the earth comes bread, but underneath it is turned by fire." We plant and do our harvests on the earth surface, but beneath the earth surface is everything that is in use on earth. And this wealth can only be discovered by searching. Thereafter, it becomes profitable only when it goes through fire. The word fire in this context speaks of pressure through sophisticated tools and machineries. If you have ever been around refinery or gold processing plants, you will understand that these products come through fire. It takes heavy pressure and fire process to bring out treasures from hidden earthly resources. The ground has to be broken into, rocks have to be cracked, and deep water has to be penetrated to access great wealth deposited therein. That is why the Bible refers to it as the shadow of death. It is the shadow of death because it is hidden in the dark places of the earth, and those with shallow knowledge cannot access it.

Verse 6 says, 'Its stones are the source of sapphires, and it contains gold dust."

Verse 7 says, 'That path no bird knows, nor the falcon's eye seen it.'

Proverbs 25 verse 2 says, 'It is the glory of God to conceal a thing, but the glory of kings to search out.

Job 10 verse 24 says, "He puts his hand on the flint, he overturns the mountain at the roots, he cuts out channels in the rocks, and his eye sees every precious thing. Verse (11) says, He binds the flood from overflowing, and the thing that is hidden he brings forth to light."

From this Scripture we can see that research, exploration and innovations are divinely ordained for human growth and wellbeing. But in the absence of visionary leaders, citizens are subjected to pain.

Verse 12 of that Scripture (Job 28) ask the rhetorical question, "But where can wisdom be found? And where is the place of understanding?

We can clearly see that it requires wisdom and understanding for a nation to embark on advanced exploration, discovering and bringing into light the abundant wealth beneath the earth.

Proverbs chapter 8 verse 11 says, "For wisdom is better than rubies, and all the things that may be desired are not to be compared to it. Wisdom speaks in verse 12 saying, "I wisdom dwell with prudence, and find out knowledge of witty inventions."

With the glaring challenges before us, and leaders dangling our nations in perils amidst plenty resources and talents, it is clear that wisdom and understanding for inventions is too expensive and unachievable for the ox because the ox lacks wisdom and understanding.

"And they sought to lay hands on Him, but feared the multitude, for they knew He had spoken the parable against them. So they left Him and went away" Mark 12:12 (NKJV).

I am hidden in Christ Jesus and standing in the company of angels and the host of heaven, to frustrate any senseless ox leader and fruitless fig that may want to attack the messenger of truth… in Jesus name, Amen!

About the Author

Andrew Robert is a Nigerian who has served in many countries as a missionary. A prolific writer with some interesting titles to his name. He is the author of "His beauty for my ashes, Don't kill this child, Gain from my garbage and commanding destiny".. all his books are available on Amazon, barnes & noble and other online platforms. With the host of other great pastors, Andrew is currently serving under Rev. Dr. Eric Nwachukwu, a great personality and Senior Pastor CGMi Church Aglow, Asaba, Nigeria. By the will of God, Andrew has his spiritual covering under a man of uncommon grace, Brother Joshua Iginla, founder Champions Royal Assembly.

Printed by Libri Plureos GmbH in Hamburg, Germany